*Praise for the
Shifters Unbound Series
By Jennifer Ashley*

### Pride Mates

With her usual gift for creating imaginative plots fueled by scorchingly sensual chemistry, RITA Award–winning Ashley begins a new sexy paranormal series that neatly combines high-adrenaline suspense with humor.
— *Booklist*

A whole new way to look at shapeshifters . . . Rousing action and sensually charged, Mapquest me the directions for Shiftertown.
— *Publishers Weekly,* "Beyond Her Book" blog

Absolutely fabulous! . . . Paranormal fans will be raving over this one!
— *The Romance Readers Connection*

### Primal Bonds

[A] sexually charged and imaginative tale . . . [A] quick pace and smart, skilled writing.
— *Publishers Weekly*

### Wild Cat

Danger, desire, and sizzling-hot action! *Wild Cat* is a wild ride.
— Alyssa Day, *New York Times* bestselling author

D0596361

# BODYGUARD

## SHIFTERS UNBOUND

## JENNIFER ASHLEY

# Chapter One

The store's owner had short and sassy black hair with a few red streaks, a compact but curvy body, and a fine-lined tattoo peeking over the collar of her shirt. Her blue eyes right now were wide as she contemplated the gun barrel aimed across the counter at her.

Ronan ducked his huge bulk back down behind the aisle partition, where he'd been crouching to examine merchandise on the bottom shelf. The robber hadn't noted Ronan, who'd come in to do some late-night shopping, almost hidden at the back of the SoCo novelty store. Ronan was willing to bet that the store's owner, Elizabeth, didn't remember at the moment that he was there either.

It was just the three of them on this Friday night: Elizabeth, the robber with the gun, and Ronan, who started making his way noiselessly toward the front counter. Ronan didn't dare charge while the gun was almost against Elizabeth's nose—one wrong move, one sound, and Elizabeth was dead.

*Wait for it.*

The robber wasn't much more than a kid; maybe twenty as humans figured age. Would be still a cub if he were Shifter. Humans couldn't control their young, Ronan thought in disgust. He'd have taken down any cub that even contemplated carrying a gun, let alone robbing a store.

Elizabeth had her hands flat on the counter. Ronan smelled her fear but also her rage. This was one of the few stores that allowed Shifters inside it, so Ronan knew a little bit about her from the Shifters who regularly shopped here. The human woman Elizabeth Chapman owned this store and worked it with her younger sister, Mabel. The store and the money in it were all they had.

*Just stall him, sweetie. Don't do anything stupid.*

The man put a shoulder bag on the counter. "Put the money in there. All of it."

"I only have about two hundred dollars." Elizabeth's voice was shaky, but Ronan heard the desperate edge to it. She was going to try to bluff him.

"I didn't ask you how much you *had*, bitch. I said put it in the bag. Then we'll check your safe."

*Give him the cash,* Ronan willed silently. *Lead him back here.*

"I already made the night's deposits," Elizabeth said.

"Don't lie to me, *chica*. I know when you make your deposits. I've been watching you. Now put the cash in the bag."

Ronan sensed Elizabeth's pounding heart, scented her fear sharpening over the oily smell of the arrogant young man. The kid wasn't wearing a mask or keeping out of sight of the store's cameras. That meant he didn't care if Elizabeth would be able to identify him later, which meant that either he was overconfident, or he meant to kill her and be long gone before any cops arrived.

*Not gonna happen.*

Ronan heard rustling as Elizabeth put the cash in the shoulder bag. "That's it," Elizabeth said. "See?"

"Open the damn safe."

"It isn't out here. It's in the back. In the office."

"So we go in the back."

Elizabeth made a little sound of pain, and Ronan knew the man had grabbed her. His blood boiled, the Shifter in him wanting the kill, and he almost came up roaring. *Not yet. Not yet.* But the bastard would pay for hurting her.

Elizabeth and her robber went by the end of the aisle, the guy carrying his shoulder bag, his gun shoved into Elizabeth's side. The look on Elizabeth's face was blank, resigned. She thought she was about to die. She didn't look around at the faint sound of Ronan shucking his jeans; never turned her head to spy him in the shadows, ready to shift. The robber kept his gaze straight ahead, focused on the office door and the potential money behind it.

Elizabeth fumbled with her keys, unlocked the door, and opened it. The lights were off. The robber shoved Elizabeth inside in front of him and let go of her long enough to reach for the light switch.

*That's my cue.*

Ronan shifted, and charged.

Elizabeth heard a small sound then felt a rush of air as something huge barreled at her in deadly silence. She saw a giant face, a massive ruff of fur, an open maw, a collar around a gigantic neck, and wide dark eyes with murder in them.

The robber, a young man with black hair and dark eyes, still had his hand on the light switch. In the next instant, the doorframe and wall around it splintered, and the robber found himself knocked to the floor with a Kodiak bear on top of him.

Elizabeth scrambled to her desk, grabbed the pepper spray she kept in her drawer, and snatched her cell phone out of her pocket at the same time. She turned around, but stopped, watching in shock as the young man struggled against all odds with the colossal bear on her Victorian pile rug.

The robber's gun went off with a *boom* of noise. Elizabeth screamed. The bear roared, the sound shaking the walls, and blood splattered to spray the floor.

The bear drew back a paw with six-inch claws and backhanded the robber across the face. The guy's head rocked. Still he fought, and the bear struck again. This time, the young man went limp, slumping to Elizabeth's rug in an ungainly heap.

The bear climbed to his feet, swung his great head around, and fixed red-raged eyes on Elizabeth.

He was the biggest living creature Elizabeth had ever seen. On all fours, the bear stood about six feet tall at the shoulder, which put his head well above Elizabeth's. His breath huffed between immense and sharp teeth, his growls rumbling from his throat like thunder. His gaze still locked on hers, he took a step toward her on one massive paw.

Elizabeth brought her hand up, aimed the can of pepper spray at his face, and gave him a full dose.

The bear blinked, drew back, blinked again, sat down on his hind legs, and rocked his head all the way back. Then he *sneezed*.

The noise exploded into the room like a sonic boom, vibrating papers on the desk and rattling the Victorian prints on the walls in their prim and proper frames.

The bear rose on his hind legs again and kept rising, ten feet — twelve — fifteen, his bulk hunching to fit under the low ceiling. At the same time, his immense body started to shrink. The bear's face contorted, muzzle shortening, as did, thank God, his teeth.

In about thirty seconds the bear was gone, and a man stood in its place. The man was just as massive as the bear — at least seven feet tall, with chocolate brown hair buzzed short, eyes as dark as the bear's, an almost square face with a once-broken nose, and a chin and jaw dark with five o'clock shadow.

His arm bore a bloody gash where the bullet had whipped by it, but his body was muscle on top of muscle on top of muscle, not an ounce of fat that Elizabeth could see. And Elizabeth saw it all, because the man was stark naked. Except for the Collar, which had shrunk to fit his human neck, the bear-man wore not a stitch.

He wiped his streaming eyes. "Shit, woman," he said in a voice that brought down a trickle of ceiling tile dust to whiten his hair. "That *itches*."

# Chapter Two

Elizabeth Chapman's red-streaked hair was mussed and her blue eyes were filled with fear as she faced Ronan, but she kept her hand firmly on the pepper spray.

"Who are you?" she demanded.

"Ronan. At your service." Ronan raised his hand in a mock salute, and blood from the bullet wound pattered to her pretty carpet. "Why'd you hit me with the pepper spray?"

Said pepper spray didn't move. "Why'd you keep coming at me, looking like you wanted to kill me?"

"I didn't. I was fighting my Collar, trying to keep it from going off. Hurts like a bitch when it does." He put out his hand and lowered the pepper spray without taking it away from her. "Now I know what stops it. Pepper spray." He shook his head again. "Shit."

"Sorry," Elizabeth said, not sounding very sorry.

"Don't worry, sweetheart. I only go after bad guys." Ronan gazed with contempt at the human stretched out on the rose-patterned rug, which now contained extra red blotches from Ronan's wound. Unconscious, the robber looked very young.

Elizabeth snatched tissues from a box on her desk and handed them to Ronan. "He shot you. You need a hospital."

Ronan took the tissues and started wiping the blood from his arm. "Grazed me, and hospitals don't know what to do with Shifters. You gonna call the cops before he wakes up?"

Elizabeth stared at the cell phone in her hand as though surprised to find it there, then she turned around and punched in the three numbers.

Ronan lifted the pistol from the floor and held it between his thumb and forefinger. He hated guns. Any projectile weapon, in fact. He guided Elizabeth out of the office as she started babbling to the 9-1-1 operator, then he set the pistol on the nearest counter and started looking for his clothes.

He found the jeans he'd tossed into the corner and pulled these back on, but his shirt, which had shredded with his swift change, was a total loss. He rummaged the nearby racks and pulled out the biggest T-shirt he could find, a bright red one with *Red-Hot Lover: Handle with Care* printed on the front.

Elizabeth still had her cell phone to her ear. "You all right?" she asked Ronan, her gaze going to the wound.

Ronan shrugged. "Will be."

"Here. They don't want me to hang up."

Elizabeth handed him the open phone, snatched some paper towels and a first-aid kit from behind the counter, and gently dabbed residual blood from his triceps. Ronan liked the brush of her slim fingers as she fixed a gauze bandage over the wound, the smell of her hair under his nose. Strawberries and honey. *Bears like honey.*

"Thanks," he rumbled.

"What were you doing in here, anyway?" Elizabeth asked as she closed the first-aid kit.

"Shopping. This is a store. I needed to buy a birthday present."

"This late?" It was going on midnight.

"Only time I had free." He growled into the cell phone. "Hey, will you guys be here any time soon? This lady needs to go home."

As though in answer, red and blue lights flashed outside, and the shop soon filled with police and paramedics. They made their way into the back office and found the inert robber, and the paramedics bundled him up and carried him out.

One of the police—a woman with black hair pulled into a hard bun and a take-no-shit stare— handed the kid's pistol and shoulder bag full of Elizabeth's money to her colleague and stayed behind to ask questions. Elizabeth described what had happened, and the female cop eyed Ronan in suspicion.

"Name," she said to him.

"Ronan."

"Ronan what?"

"Just Ronan. Bears don't have surnames."

The police officer had a smooth face and cold, black eyes. "You're a Shifter," she said.

"No kidding." Ronan glanced at Elizabeth, whose lips were too bloodless. "Can you let her go home? She's pretty shaken up."

"After she gives me her statement. You too, Shifter. In fact, I want you coming in with us."

She put away her little notebook and took out a pair of cuffs. They were big cuffs, and Ronan saw the markings that told him they had Fae magic in them, fashioned to contain Shifters.

"What are you doing?" Elizabeth asked, wide-eyed. "Ronan didn't rob me. He helped me."

"He's a Shifter," the woman said. "He hit a human, and the human's going to the hospital. That's assault, and for Shifters a capital crime. I have to arrest him." *Rules are rules,* her flat eyes seemed to say.

"You mean that he hit a human who was about to kill me," Elizabeth said heatedly. "If Ronan hadn't been here, I'd be dead."

The officer shrugged. "If you want to come down and plead his case to the judge, it's your choice. But I have to take him."

Ronan saw indecision flicker in Elizabeth Chapman's eyes. This wasn't her fight. She wanted to go home and forget about the robbery as best she could. Ronan wasn't sure what human females did to make themselves feel better, but the cub, Cherie, who lived in his house, liked to take baths that lasted forever whenever she was stressed. Which was often, considering what she'd gone through.

Ronan's fantasies went to Elizabeth in a bathtub, her curved body covered with suds, her black hair wet. He bet she looked cute with her hair all damp and spiky.

The cop clicked the cuffs onto Ronan's wrists behind his back, and the pleasant vision dissolved as he felt the sting of Fae magic. Even the small bite of it ground through his nerves and tried to set off a spark from his Collar. Elizabeth looked concerned as he winced, but Ronan shook his head at her.

"Don't worry about me, Lizzie-girl. But do me a favor. Find a lawyer called Kim Fraser — she's mated to Liam Morrissey in Shiftertown, and they live next door to Glory. I know you know Glory — she comes in here all the time. Tell Kim what happened for me?"

Kim, a human, had set up a law office that specialized in helping Shifters. Because human laws governing Shifters were restrictive and complex, Shifters needed all the help they could get.

"All right?" Ronan repeated, looking hard at Elizabeth. "Tell her?"

Elizabeth pressed her slim hands together and held them a little under her chin. Human body language for *I don't know what the right thing is to do here.*

"You can call her if you don't want to go to Shiftertown," Ronan said. "Her card's in my front pocket."

Ronan's hands were locked behind his back and staying there. Elizabeth took a step forward. The female cop didn't say or do anything, just watched, ready to take down both of them if they tried anything stupid.

Elizabeth's hair smelled good. So did the rest of her. Ronan scented Elizabeth's residual fear from the robbery, overlaid with the warm goodness of her, and behind that, concern for someone else. Layers of scent that told him all about her.

He liked how she'd put the red streaks in her hair. Defiance—that's what it meant. Elizabeth seemed like a good businesswoman, following the rules, but those little streaks said she could be bad if she wanted to be. Or maybe they were a reminder of a time when she hadn't walked the straight and narrow. Ronan thought he wouldn't mind a glimpse of the bad-ass Elizabeth.

Elizabeth dipped her fingers into Ronan's front pocket. She did it quickly and competently, not touching Ronan at all as she plucked out Kim's business card. The move was practiced, as though she'd gotten good at taking things out of people's pockets. *Skill* was the word. Interesting.

"I'll call her," Elizabeth said, palming the card. "But I'm coming down to the station with you," she said to the cop. "He helped me, and it's not fair he's getting arrested when some gang kid tried to kill me."

The female cop shrugged. "Suit yourself. Come on, Shifter."

Ronan winked as the cop took his arm in a practiced grip and shoved him out the door. "I like you, human woman," he said to Elizabeth. "See you downtown."

\*\*\* \*\*\* \*\*\*

Elizabeth called Mabel, reassuring her sister that everything was all right, then reached Kim Fraser on the phone and told her what had happened.

She then drove her small pickup downtown, following the cops to the jail and courthouse. She found it ironic that she had to leave her truck in a crappy lot with a sign saying *Park at your own risk,* while the arrests for the night were taken safely around to the front door.

Inside the station, Elizabeth gave her official statement to the female cop, then was told to stay in the waiting room until someone came to take her to Ronan's hearing. She hadn't thought the hearing would be tonight, not this late, but apparently Shifter Division processed Shifters as swiftly as possible.

So Elizabeth waited. Around her, arrests for the night were brought in, anything from indecent exposure to grand theft auto to assault with a deadly weapon. This was the heart of Texas, in a well-populated county, and the arrestees ranged from men with shaggy hair, baseball caps, and strong South Texas accents; to Spanish-speaking kids who glared in fearful defiance; to brightly dressed prostitutes with hair of every shade and shorts cut high up their butts.

Elizabeth had never been in this particular police station, but they all gave her the creeps. The smell was the same—burned coffee, body odor, and floor cleaner overlaid with stale cigarette smoke. Smoking was no longer permitted inside, but the smoke clung to the clothes of people who went in and out.

Never again, she'd vowed. For Mabel's sake. Elizabeth had half-feared that the female cop would run a check on Elizabeth's name, but then, even if she had, the woman would have found nothing. Elizabeth Chapman had no criminal record, and no connection to anyone with a criminal record. Elizabeth had made sure of that.

After a long time, a tall black bailiff stopped in front of Elizabeth and said in a booming voice, "Ms. Chapman? Come with me."

Elizabeth sprang up and followed the man, half-running to keep up with his long-legged stride. "Where are we going?"

"The Shifter's hearing," was all he would say.

The bailiff led Elizabeth through a door and down a hall that was eerily deserted. At the end of this, he unbolted and unlocked a steel door that had to be a foot thick. He took Elizabeth into a short hall, maybe five feet in length, which had no other door but the one at its far end.

Why was Elizabeth reminded of zoo cages? The kind with two doors and a space in between, where an animal could be trapped if it tried to escape. The bailiff unlocked the second door, also of foot-thick steel, and ushered Elizabeth into a long, narrow courtroom.

It was a courtroom unlike any Elizabeth had seen, and unfortunately she'd seen quite a few during her colorful adolescence. The judge's bench, at the far end, was raised six feet off the floor and caged in front by floor-to-ceiling iron bars. A woman in judge's robes was just coming through a door right behind the bench. Bench, door, and judge were unreachable by anyone on the courtroom floor.

Ronan sat in a large metal chair below the bench, at a right angle to the rest of the room. His hands were now shackled in front of him; a chain between the shackles hooked them to a ring on the heavy chair, which in turn was bolted to the floor.

The courtroom was unadorned, no paneling on the walls, no heavy wooden tables or carved benches, just a generic linoleum floor, white walls, and two plain metal benches in the front of the room. A nervous man in a suit, probably the prosecutor, occupied the right bench. A man and woman sat together on the bench on the left.

The woman was human, with short dark hair, a business jacket and skirt, and a briefcase. Her buttoned-up look screamed lawyer, though she wore sandals on bare feet instead of hose and shoes.

The man next to her was a Shifter, no doubt about it. He had dark hair, eyes of incredible blue, and a Collar around his neck. He lounged on the bench, watching everyone in the room, including the judge, with an air of command.

Most people believed that Shifters posed a threat to humans, and looking at this man, Elizabeth finally understood why. Ronan was huge and full of muscle, but this Shifter, while nowhere near as big as Ronan, exuded a strength of presence that spoke of power. No matter that he wore a Collar, he could be deadly, and he wanted everyone around him to remember that.

Ronan saw Elizabeth and lifted his shackled hands in greeting. He looked the calmest of anyone in the room, no matter that they were treating him like a dangerous animal.

Granted, Elizabeth had seen Ronan as a big, scary bear, and even now, with his buzzed hair, glittering eyes, and muscles bulging out the *Red-Hot Lover* T-shirt, he still looked frightening. But he gave her a nod—in thanks, she guessed, for calling Kim and then showing up herself.

The tall bailiff locked the door, the clang of the keys loud. The judge hammered once with her gavel. "Counsels approach the bench."

That was it. No one else apparently would show up to this hearing, no court stenographer, no other witnesses. Maybe the session was being recorded, but what did Elizabeth know? Perhaps records weren't kept of Shifter hearings.

As Kim rose with the prosecutor and walked confidently toward the judge, the bailiff said to Elizabeth, "Sit over there."

He pointed to the seat next to Kim's Shifter. The Shifter sat up from his lounging position, smiled, and patted the bench next to him. The smile was charming, but it was also predatory, and his eyes were watching, watching. Ronan caught Elizabeth's worried look and sent her another nod.

Elizabeth went to the bench. The Shifter rose, though both judge and bailiff scowled at him, and stuck out his hand. "I'm Liam Morrissey," he said. "You're Elizabeth?"

"Elizabeth Chapman. I called your wife."

"She's my mate." Liam closed his right hand around Elizabeth's and then laid his left hand on top of it, sandwiching her fingers in a cushion of warmth. Liam Morrissey was the leader of the Austin Shiftertown, Elizabeth knew. He and his wife—no, *mate*—Kim, were the liaisons between Shifters and humans. "No worries, lass," Liam said. "You answer the judge's questions and tell the truth. Kim will take care of the rest."

The pressure of his hands on hers and the confident look in his eyes, together with the Irish lilt to his voice, were soothing and reassuring. Elizabeth found herself nodding, wanting to promise she'd do her best.

Ronan said from across the room, "You can let go of her now, Liam."

Liam's smile widened but he released Elizabeth. "I'm thinking you're growing a mite possessive, my friend," he said to Ronan.

"I'm thinking she's had a bad night," Ronan growled. "That and I can break your head with one hand."

"Shut it, Bear. I'm mate-bonded. You have no competition from me."

The judge pounded with her gavel. "The defendant will stay in order," she said sharply. Both Ronan and Liam went quiet but neither looked contrite.

*The Shifters are in charge here,* Elizabeth realized. *Not the judge, not the bailiff, not the prosecutor. Liam and Ronan might be inside the cage, but they've taken it over.*

"The defendant will approach," the judge said.

The bailiff unlocked Ronan's shackles from the chair, helped him stand, and led him forward. Kim came to Ronan's side, not looking worried, though the prosecutor kept his eyes on his notes as Ronan hulked next to him.

"The charge is assault with intent to kill a human," the judge said. She had dark hair going to gray, a face like a squashed prune, and a flat voice. "How does the defendant plead?"

"He pleads mitigating circumstances," Kim said. "And intent to kill is not on the arrest sheet. The human in question was armed with a loaded nine-millimeter pistol. My client was defending the owner of the store the human man had come to rob and was shot by the human in the process."

The judge eyed Kim in dislike. "I asked for the plea, not the defense. You'll have the chance to speak in a moment. Prosecution?"

The prosecutor finally looked up from his file folder. "The victim, Julio Marquez, is at the hospital being treated for claw wounds. Mr. Marquez describes being attacked by a bear in Ms. Chapman's shop on South Congress. In fear for his life, Mr. Marquez shot but missed. The bear then struck Mr. Marquez again, rendering him unconscious. According to Mr. Marquez, he entered the store on a dare by his friends and waved around his gun. The bear attacked from the back of the store. Mr. Marquez did not see him before that."

Elizabeth jumped to her feet. "That's not what happened!" A dare by his friends? No way in hell. Elizabeth had looked into the cold, hard eyes of the kid, which had held an anger too old for his age. She'd recognized that anger. Julio Marquez was a dangerous young man.

The judge banged her gavel. "Ms. Chapman, sit down, or you will be fined for contempt."

The prosecutor leafed through his file. "Mr. Marquez's statement and Ms. Chapman's are not exactly the same, but both agree that the bear attacked Mr. Marquez."

"Because Marquez was forcing me into my office at gunpoint!" Elizabeth cried.

Another steely glare from the judge. "You will be called to give your version of events in due time, Ms. Chapman. Sit *down*."

"Best sit down, love," Liam whispered. "Kim will take care of it."

He sounded confident. Elizabeth sank to the bench, and Liam nodded at her. *Good girl.* Ronan sent her another reassuring look over his shoulder.

Even Kim seemed unperturbed. "The witness is understandably stressed, Your Honor," she said. "It's late, and she's had a bad experience."

The judge really didn't like Kim Fraser. For defending a Shifter? Elizabeth wondered. Or for marrying one?

The prosecutor broke in. "Maybe Ms. Chapman should be allowed to give her evidence so she can go home."

The judge's face softened as she listened to the prosecutor. The man was attractive in a slick sort of way . . . *what a witch.*

"Of course," the judge said. "Ms. Chapman?"

At that moment, Elizabeth's cell phone pealed. She was surprised she could get a signal behind all the steel doors, but the name that popped up on the screen was Mabel's.

"Cell phones are supposed to be off," the judge snapped.

"I have to take this. It's my little sister. She's home alone, and she's worried."

The judge looked as though nothing had ever harassed her more. "Outside."

The bailiff unlocked the door. Elizabeth charged out, and Liam quietly followed her.

"Mabel? I can't talk right now, honey. I'm in court."

Mabel's frantic voice cut over hers. "Lizzy, there are men outside, trying to get in. A bunch of them, and they have guns. I don't know what to do. I'm so scared!"

# Chapter Three

"Call the police," Elizabeth yelled down the phone, watery fear pouring through her. "Call them now."

"I tried. They don't answer."

"Then you hide. I'm in a courthouse. I'll get—"

Elizabeth stifled a shriek as Liam Morrissey snatched the phone out of her hand. "Mabel? This is Liam Morrissey. Connor's uncle, that's right. You rest easy, now, lass. I'll take care of this. Stay down, behind a bed, don't go near the windows. My lads will be there before you can count to ten. All right?"

He clicked off the connection and dialed another with ease of long practice. While Elizabeth stood there with her mouth open, Liam said quietly into the phone, "Sean, get Dad and Spike and go up to Thirty-Fifth Street near MoPac. Mabel Chapman. She's got armed intruders. Go *now*."

Whoever was on the other end hung up, but Liam kept hold of the phone. "Now, don't you worry. My brother will take care of your sister. Let's go back and get Ronan sprung."

Elizabeth didn't move. "I can't. I have to go home."

Liam put a warm hand on her shoulder. "You going home would only put you in danger as well. My brother and my trackers can help Mabel better than the police. No one stops my trackers, lass. No one. Come on, now."

Liam had reassurance down to a science. In spite of her gut-wrenching fear, Elizabeth let him lead her back past the bailiff and once more into the courtroom.

"Oh, I see that you're still with us, Ms. Chapman," the judge said. "How nice. Please approach and read the words on the card."

Elizabeth promised to tell the truth and the whole truth, so help her God, then went over her story, prompted by questions from the prosecutor. It was like being in a play—she might not know her lines, but the prosecutor wanted her to say certain ones, judging from his cues. Ronan, back in the chair, leaned forward, resting his big arms on his knees, watching her closely.

Fear for Mabel gnawed at Elizabeth as she answered the questions. Liam still had her cell phone. He glanced at it from time to time, his face grim.

Elizabeth concluded shakily, "So I know that if Ronan hadn't been there, Marquez would have killed me."

"But you don't actually know that," the prosecutor said in his condescending way. "That's only what you guess."

That did it. The gloves came off. "Look, I grew up with kids like Marquez," Elizabeth said. "Any guilt or conscience in him went away a long time ago. He only deals in *if*-then questions. *If* I can identify him, *then* he shoots me. In his mind, I was dead as soon as he walked in the door. End of story."

The prosecutor shrugged apologetically at the judge. "It's still only what she thinks."

At that point, Liam got up and went to the door again. He held a murmured exchange with the bailiff, who did not look happy, but the bailiff let him out.

"Defense counsel, any questions for the witness?" the judge asked.

So far Kim had listened with a calm look on her face, not objecting to anything the prosecutor had said. Elizabeth had stood in front of judges before — sometimes as the defendant — and a good defense counsel would have been all over the prosecutor's overly leading questions.

"I have only one, Your Honor," Kim said. She turned to Elizabeth, her face expressionless, professional. "Ms. Chapman, tell me, at any time — before, during, or even after the scuffle — did Ronan's Collar go off?"

Liam reentered the room. Behind the bailiff's back, he gave Elizabeth a thumb's up, and Elizabeth somehow knew that Mabel was all right. Her legs nearly buckled in relief. But what had Liam done?

"Ms. Chapman?" Kim asked, waiting.

"Uh — go off? What does that mean?"

Kim said, "When a Shifter tries to attack someone, the Collar around his neck shocks him. It's very obvious—you'd see a white-blue arc running all the way around the Collar, sparking like those plasma balls. The Collar causes a lot of pain and stops the Shifter. They're programmed to suppress a Shifter's instinct to kill."

Elizabeth replayed the awful scene in her mind, remembering the swift silence with which Ronan had burst through her office door. She closed her eyes and made herself remember every detail. Ronan's huge face, the Collar clasping his big neck, the power in his gigantic body as he knocked Marquez to the ground.

She opened her eyes. "No. I didn't see anything like that. The gun went off and hit Ronan, but his Collar never sparked. I think Ronan was just trying to take the weapon away from Marquez."

Kim turned back to the judge, looking as professional as ever, but with a sparkle of triumph in her eyes. "There's a whole ream of scientific data on Shifters as to why they can't commit an act of violence while they wear Collars. If the Collar didn't go off in Ms. Chapman's store, that means my client had no malicious intent toward Marquez. My client saw the danger to Ms. Chapman and stepped in to make sure she wasn't hurt, and in the scuffle to keep the gun away from Marquez, Marquez was knocked unconscious. If my client had any intent to hurt or kill, the Collar would have had him in agony, even a big man like him." Kim walked to the judge's bench, rose on tiptoe, and laid a thick folder on it. "Here are a few of the many studies done on the Collars. I can produce more if Your Honor needs them."

The judge looked irritated. She flipped the file open, flipped it closed, gave Kim a dirty look, and sent a nastier one to Ronan.

"I'm going to let your client go," she said. "Not because you make a good point, Ms. Fraser. Partly it's because Marquez has previous arrests for armed robbery, and Ms. Chapman's story is plausible, but mostly because it's late and I want you all out of my courtroom. But I'm going to tell you, Mr. Ronan, to confine yourself to Shiftertown and not leave it for one month. I don't want you anywhere near humans, understand? If you leave Shiftertown, I will have your carcass hauled in front of me again, and then you won't walk out of here so easily."

"Begging Your Honor's pardon." Liam Morrissey shot her his charming grin. "Ronan's job lies outside Shiftertown, just outside the gates, in fact. He works for me, and he supports three kiddies with his salary. It would be a great hardship on his family if he couldn't go to his job."

"Fine." The judge scowled, but even she wasn't immune to Liam's smile. "He goes to work, then right back home. Consider him under house arrest. I'm holding you responsible for him." The judge pointed her gavel at Liam then banged it on the bench. She got up, robes swirling, and stalked out through the door behind the bench, which closed with a bang.

Elizabeth was bursting to ask Liam what had happened at her house, but she had to wait for the bailiff to unlock Ronan from his shackles and then unlock the doors to let them out. Both Ronan and Kim had to sign things after that, and then they all had to walk out of the courthouse, back to the dark streets outside.

"What about my sister?" Elizabeth nearly shouted at Liam as soon as they cleared the front door.

Ronan put a large hand on Elizabeth's shoulder, but it was comforting, not heavy. Kim walked close to her other side.

"Mabel's fine, lass," Liam said. "My brother and dad got there in time. They and my trackers scared the bad guys away."

"What bad guys? Why were they trying to break into my house?"

They started down the street to the nearly deserted parking lot a half block away. Only two vehicles stood in the lot: Elizabeth's small pickup and a sweet-looking Harley.

"I don't know," Liam said. "Sean only told me that your sister was safe and that the trackers were sniffing around, seeing what they can find out."

"Trackers—you said that before. What trackers?"

"The trackers work for Liam," Ronan said. "They're guards, finders, warriors. Some of them can be complete assholes, but they're the best at what they do."

"Nothing will happen to Mabel with my trackers looking out for her," Liam said. "I promise you that."

Elizabeth closed her eyes a brief moment in relief. "Thank you, Mr. Morrissey."

"Yeah, thanks, Liam," Ronan said. "And you, Kim. Especially you."

Ronan shouldered Liam out of the way and snatched Kim into a big hug. *A bear hug*, Elizabeth thought, feeling a little hysterical. Kim hugged him in return, and Liam stood by, not seeming to mind the large man holding on to his wife.

Kim patted Ronan's back. "You're welcome, big guy. Can I breathe now?"

Ronan released her and stepped back, then damned if he didn't turn and enclose Liam in the same kind of hug. Elizabeth watched, eyes widening, as Liam wrapped his arms around the bigger man and held him close.

"You get used to it after a while," Kim said. Her nose wrinkled with her smile. "Sort of."

Liam and Ronan broke apart. Liam reached for his wife—no, his *mate*. Elizabeth was never going to get used to these terms. Liam hugged Kim and kissed her firmly on the mouth, and then he turned to Elizabeth and Ronan, one arm securely around Kim.

"Take her home, Ronan."

Elizabeth blinked. "What? He can't. He was put under house arrest ten minutes ago. That doesn't include driving across town to my house."

Ronan stood very close to Elizabeth. She could feel the heat from his body, remembered the feel of the powerful bear rushing past her in his intense and deadly charge. Ronan had saved her life, tonight. His Collar might not have gone off, but no matter what Elizabeth had told the judge, the bear in him had been ready to kill. Elizabeth had seen the need for murder in men's eyes before, and Ronan had definitely had it.

"No room for me on Liam's Harley," Ronan said. "I'll have to go with you."

Liam and Kim had already mounted the motorcycle, Liam leaving the rest of the arrangements up to Ronan and Elizabeth.

"All right, you have a point," Elizabeth said. "But I'll take *you* back to Shiftertown and then drive myself home."

"Whatever." Ronan held out his hand. "Keys."

"What? No. It's not like I'm drunk." *Yet*.

"After the night you've had? Nope. I'm driving you. "

Elizabeth felt sick and stretched, her head ached, and her eyes felt hollow. She needed about a gallon of water and then one of coffee, a long bath, a hot toddy, and a really good night's sleep. *After* she made sure Mabel was safe.

"Fine." She dropped the keys into Ronan's hand.

"Cool." He snapped his fingers around them. "I've always wanted to drive one of these little pickups. Don't tell anyone."

The Harley roared to life. Liam lifted his hand and so did Kim, then Liam pulled out into the night. Kim, helmeted, leaned into Liam's back, as though she loved him body and soul. A human and a Shifter. What a crazy night.

Ronan opened the passenger door and got Elizabeth inside. "I'm supposed to like muscle cars. Strongman, macho cars." He shut her door and went around to the driver's side. He barely fit behind the wheel and had to slide the seat all the way back. "Monster trucks. Bad-ass motorcycles. Anything big and chunky that makes a lot of noise. Nothing cute and girlie. So keep this quiet. Deal?"

Now he was making her laugh. "Your secret is safe with me."

Not that Ronan could ever be mistaken for cute and girlie. He was huge but solid, like a pro wrestler, tall but perfectly proportional. His face wasn't exactly handsome—too hard for that, and he'd had his nose and right cheekbone broken at some time in his past. But his face was striking. His eyes were dark brown, almost black, but not cold. They were warm, very warm.

Ronan started up the truck and peeled out of the parking lot. Elizabeth held on as he raced around a corner and pulled onto Seventh heading due east.

Elizabeth wanted to talk to Mabel, to reassure her sister that she was on her way home. She reached for her phone and found an empty place on her belt. "Oh, crap. Liam still has my cell phone."

"Not surprised. Liam likes gadgets. He'll give it back to you when he's done with it."

"Doesn't he have his own?"

"Sure, but Shifters don't get to have fancy smart phones. Our phones call and hang up, that's it. I bet he's texting every human he knows, or playing games, or taking pictures. He's like a cub when he gets a new gadget in his hand. But I'll make him give it back."

Ronan drove through the sparse traffic as he spoke, flashed under the I-35, and sped on in entirely the opposite direction from Elizabeth's house.

"Where are you going?" she asked. "I live northwest of downtown."

"You're not going home," Ronan said, gripping the wheel as he spun the truck around another corner.

"I'm not?" Her trepidation returned. "Why not?"

Ronan looked over at her and grinned. It was a warm grin, making his eyes twinkle. "Because I'm taking you to my home, Elizabeth Chapman. *Shiftertown*."

# Chapter Four

Ronan felt Elizabeth's fear pouring off her as they neared the streets of Shiftertown. But there was nothing frightening about Shiftertown—at least, not these days.

When Ronan had first arrived from Alaska, though, he'd been scared as hell. Bears liked solitude, and Ronan had never lived near more than one or two people at a time in his life. In Shiftertown, scores of Shifters surrounded him, always. And then the human government had told him he had to let other bears live in the same *house* with him.

Ronan's shyness had nearly killed him. Learning to survive the discomfort of being in a crowd, training himself to not react—either by running away or driving the others off—had been the hardest thing Ronan had done. People who derided shyness, or called it self-centeredness, didn't understand it. Shyness was instinct. In the wild, the need for personal space—a lot of personal space—could spell the difference between survival and death.

But Ronan had conquered his fear long ago, thank the Goddess. Now Ronan knew everyone, and everyone knew Ronan, and he'd carved out his own place in this strange, new world.

Ronan drove around a dark corner that contained a deserted convenience store and headed into Shiftertown. Beyond an empty lot, which was purposely left derelict, Shiftertown unrolled in streets of neat lawns and well-kept bungalows.

These houses had been pretty much trashed and abandoned by the humans who'd lived there twenty years before, and the government department formed to deal with the Shifter situation had snapped up the cheap real estate and used it to house the Shifters. Shifters had moved in and repainted, reshingled, and repaired the houses themselves. Now anyone could walk fearlessly down the quiet streets of Shiftertown, doors could remain unlocked, and cubs could play safely in the front yards to all hours of the night.

Shifters, three species of them, now lived together without killing each other. Who would have thought?

Shiftertown was dark this late, though windows glowed in houses here and there. Felines and Lupines would be outside without lights, both species still nocturnal despite human effort to change that. Bears, much smarter, would be sound asleep, taking advantage of every moment of shut-eye they could get. Ursines used a lot of energy when awake, and they slept with dedication.

Elizabeth, beside him, took it all in while gripping the dashboard. "Are you going to bother to tell me why I'm in Shiftertown?"

"Sean brought your sister here, to my house."

She whipped around to stare at him. "To *your* house? Why?"

"Well, he couldn't take her to Liam's house because Connor lives there, and that could get messy. Mabel likes Connor, but Connor's still a cub."

Elizabeth kept staring at him, clearly having no idea what he was talking about. "If you mean Connor who comes into my shop sometimes to flirt with Mabel, he's not a cub; he's in college."

"He's only twenty-one, and in Shifter terms, that's still a cub. Won't make his Transition for another, oh, seven or eight years yet. It's best not to let him and Mabel be more than friends — too confusing and even dangerous for everyone. So, right now, my house is best. You've heard the story of Goldilocks and the Three Bears?"

"Sure, but what has that got to do with —"

"That story is total bullshit." Ronan laughed, the rumble of it filling the truck. "At my house, nothing's too hard or too soft. Everything is *just right.* "

He was rewarded with Elizabeth's smile. He liked her smile, like a sudden flash of sunshine. He hated to see her so afraid. She shouldn't be afraid, this sassy sweetheart.

Ronan slowed the truck, which he'd found fun to drive but a tight fit. He turned into the driveway, which was nothing but two strips of broken pavement that led behind the house. Ronan had turned the garage in the back into a work-and-play room he and his housemates called the Den, so he parked outside, behind the other car and a large motorcycle already there.

The motorcycle was Ronan's—Sean or a tracker must have retrieved it from the street near Elizabeth's store and driven it home for him. He hoped it hadn't been Nate who'd fetched it. Stupid Feline drove like an idiot.

Ronan got out before Elizabeth could and went around to open her door. "Here we are," he said, taking her hand to help her stand up. He liked her hand, small and warm in his. "Get ready for the horde."

"The what?"

"No worries; I won't let them hurt you."

The "horde" tumbled out of the back door and off the porch Ronan had built around two sides of the house. They were Rebecca, a full-grown she-bear from Ronan's clan; Scott, a black bear Shifter who was about twenty-seven and going through the pains of his Transition; Cherie, a grizzly, twenty in human years, who'd spent the first half of her life locked in a pen. Last came Olaf, the only polar bear in Shiftertown, nine in human years and still a true cub. Olaf had a sunny disposition, except when flashes of the past he couldn't quite remember came to him in his dreams. They called him Olaf, but no one, not even Olaf, knew his real name. All wore Collars that gleamed under the porch lights.

Behind the bears was Mabel, Elizabeth's twenty-one-year-old sister, whose hair today was pink streaked with green. She looked keyed up, frightened, and excited, all at the same time. She pushed past the bears and ran at Elizabeth, arms open.

"Lizzy, damn it, they said you almost got shot, and then you were at that police station for, like, ever. And then those guys came to our house—looking for you. They called through the front door asking where you were. And then Shifters, all over the place. Liam said it wasn't safe for me to stay home, said I would meet up with you here. Have you seen that Spike guy? He is *hot*. I swear he has tattoos *everywhere*."

Sounded like Mabel was all right then.

Rebecca looked at Ronan in concern. "Ronan? Liam said you took a bullet. You all right?"

Ronan held up his arm to show her the gauze bandage. "I'm fine. It just grazed me." A tiny bullet cutting across Ronan's triceps was nothing. He'd been shot with a Fae arrow last year—now that had *hurt*. The effing Fae spelled their arrows.

"You were jumping in front of bullets again, weren't you, Ronan?" Cherie said, folding her arms. She had black-and-brown streaked hair, entirely natural, matching her grizzly's coat. "You've gotta stop that. We need you without holes."

"Leave him alone," Scott said. "He did what he had to do."

Scott was a black bear, the smallest of the horde when he shifted, but he was still tall and lanky, with black hair and a surly expression. The Transition was hard on him.

Olaf was still mastering English, having been located by Liam and brought to Shiftertown only a year ago. He had white-blond hair and black eyes, and his bear was too adorable to be real. "Mabel paints my hair too. Okay, Ronan?"

"I said he'd look cute with blue streaks in his hair," Mabel said.

Rebecca shot Ronan an evil look. "I told him it was up to you."

"Sure, thanks, Becks. Not now, Olaf. This is Elizabeth, Mabel's sister. She and Mabel are staying. So keep it down so they can sleep. I'll give them my room and sleep out in the Den."

"No, no, no, don't do that to them," Rebecca said quickly. "They're taking *my* room, which is habitable, and I'll sleep in the Den. Putting them in your room would be cruel and unusual punishment."

"I'm sleeping with Rebecca," Cherie said quickly. She always felt nervous when Rebecca was out of the house.

"Whatever. Female bears," Ronan said to Elizabeth. "They like to take over. Everything."

"Hey, Papa-Bear was out being arrested," Rebecca said. "For being a knight errant. I didn't realize that was a crime in the human world."

"I did smack the guy," Ronan said. "But he deserved it. His mother must be too soft on him."

"His mother is probably terrified of him," Elizabeth said. "Or maybe she's as bad as he is, or — most likely — not there at all."

Ronan realized he still had hold of Elizabeth's hand. He also realized he wasn't in that big a hurry to let it go. Rebecca noticed, but — thank the Goddess — kept her thoughts to herself.

"How do you know so much about humans like Marquez?" Ronan asked Elizabeth. "You said in the courtroom you knew exactly what he was going to do."

Mabel rolled her eyes before Elizabeth could answer. "You do *not* want to know. Elizabeth was a juvenile delinquent. In a big way."

"I thought they didn't want to know." Elizabeth shook off Ronan's hand. "It's nice of you, Ronan, but we can't stay here. I don't have a change of clothes, for one thing."

"I brought your stuff," Mabel said brightly. "And Sean says we have to stay. He's cute, Lizzy—you should hear his Irish accent. Too bad he's mated, but I like his mate. Andrea, you've met her before. Anyway, Sean says we're staying in Shiftertown until Liam and the trackers make sure it's safe for us to go home."

Elizabeth held up her hands. "Mabel, stop talking for just a second—"

"Shiftertown's the safest place for you," Ronan broke in. "No one will find you here. The trackers will sniff around, find out what these people wanted with your house, and deal with them."

Ronan saw Rebecca's eyes flicker when he said, *Deal with them,* and the two bears shared a look. The phrase could have many shades of meaning, especially with the Morrisseys involved.

*Juvenile delinquent. In a big way.* Ronan remembered how Elizabeth had lifted the card from his pocket—quickly and skillfully. There was more to Elizabeth Chapman than met the eye, and Ronan was determined to find out all about her.

Elizabeth still hesitated, but Olaf walked up to her and put his little hand in hers. "Inside," he said in his thickly accented English. "We keep you safe, Lizbeth."

The little cub did what all the adults could not. Elizabeth's look softened, and she let Olaf lead her into the house.

*** *** ***

Elizabeth followed Olaf, whose little hand had a surprisingly strong grip. Kids were very good at giving off danger signals, but Olaf radiated confidence that Elizabeth would be all right in Ronan's house.

Behind her, Rebecca herded the rest of them, including Ronan, inside. She had to let Olaf help her lead Mabel and Elizabeth upstairs to her small bedroom on the second floor; Olaf would not relinquish Elizabeth's hand until she was safely inside the room.

The bedroom was neat and spare, without many personal possessions. Rebecca took some extra blankets out of a closet and spread them across the double bed. She shook her head when Elizabeth tried to thank her, then grabbed some clothes and headed out.

"Ronan's in the next room," Rebecca said in the doorway. "If his snoring gets too loud, bang on the wall. Sometimes that works." She flipped her spare shirt over her shoulder and disappeared.

The door closed. Through it Elizabeth could hear the three younger ones going back downstairs, all talking to Ronan and Rebecca at once, and Ronan's rumbling bass answering them.

"Isn't this cool?" Mabel pulled up the blinds and looked out at the dark street below. "I always wanted to come to Shiftertown. I think Connor Morrissey lives over there." She pointed.

Elizabeth sat down on the bed, her legs giving out. Everything from staring at the black opening of the gun, to trying to remember what had happened for Ronan's hearing, to the shock of being brought to Shiftertown to meet Ronan's—family?—was taking its toll.

"Are the kids his?" she asked Mabel. "And Rebecca, is she his wife? Or mate, I mean?"

"Nope." Mabel finally let down the blind and turned away from the window. "None of the kids are related to each other or to Ronan or Rebecca. Rebecca says she's Ronan's cousin or something, distant. They're not mated, and they can't mate, because they're in the same clan. Otherwise, this is like a foster home for Bear Shifters, but way better than a human one."

That was for sure.

Mabel, always resilient, stripped off her clothes and got into bed in her underwear. Mabel usually slept in the nude, so Elizabeth supposed she was keeping herself covered to be courteous to Elizabeth. She'd brought Elizabeth's nightshirt and a change of clothes in a shoulder bag, and Elizabeth pulled on the nightshirt and snuggled down against Mabel. She closed her eyes but, as she'd guessed it would, sleep evaded her.

But it wasn't the kid with the gun Elizabeth kept seeing as she lay, restless and awake. It was Ronan, first charging in to her rescue, then rising into a perfectly proportioned, hard-bodied man with muscles everywhere. He had one tatt, a Celtic interlocking pattern that laced across the small of his back. His buzzed short hair was dark brown, almost black, but with highlights of lighter brown. His bear's fur had the same rippling, rich brown color.

Tonight Elizabeth had seen him range from enraged and ready to kill, to annoyed, to resigned, to worried, to reassuring, to affectionate. Ronan might be gruff with the kids who lived with him, but she could tell he was fond of them.

Elizabeth had always had a problem with trust. For good reason—some of the people she'd ended up living with as a kid had been horrible, some dangerous. She'd done everything in her power to protect Mabel from them, which meant she'd had to make some tough choices.

The lesson Elizabeth had learned early in life was that you didn't trust anyone. For any reason. People who acted as though you could rely on them would turn on you the second they were no longer interested in your problems. You couldn't count on even the nicest people in a pinch.

So she didn't know what to make of Ronan offering her and Mabel a place to sleep, or the Shifters surging across town to get Mabel out of danger. She didn't know anything about Shifters or what drove them—or what they'd expect from her in return.

She could only do what she'd done all her life—sit tight, scope out the lay of the land, and decide what to do from there. Her eyes remained open as she thought over all this, but Mabel soon dropped off into innocent sleep, emitting faint, peaceful snores.

*** *** ***

Elizabeth left her room in the morning to the smell of coffee and bacon wafting up the stairs. Cherie was across the hall, leaning against the closed door of the one bathroom.

"Come on, Scott, does anyone else get to use the bathroom today?"

Scott's voice roared back over running water. "I'm in the shower!"

"You've been in the shower for half an hour. We have guests, you big idiot."

"I didn't ask them here!"

Cherie saw Elizabeth and rolled her eyes. "He's in Transition. It's like he can't get himself clean enough, as if *that's* going to make females fall all over him. There aren't enough female Shifters in this Shiftertown anyway—he won't have a chance to mate for years yet."

"Transition?"

"From cub to adult," Cherie said. "I hope I'm not this insensitive when it's my turn." She slapped her palm to the door. "Scott, would you quit hogging the bathroom?"

"Go next door!" he shouted.

"Males." Cherie rolled her eyes again. She was pretty, with the deep, startling beauty that Rebecca had, hers not as fully developed yet. Cherie looked about twenty in human years, only a little younger than Mabel, but apparently, like Connor, she was still considered a cub.

"Probably best you have breakfast first," Cherie said. "If there's any hot water left when he's done, you and your sister can have dibs on the bathroom."

"Whatever works," Elizabeth said, shrugging. You needed to establish territory fast in a foster home, but you also had to show that you were willing to be flexible with those who didn't fight you.

Besides, Elizabeth would be home soon, in her own bathroom.

She went down the stairs. This was an old bungalow, likely built in the 1920s or 30s, laid out in a square with the staircase in the middle. It was pretty big, as far as bungalows went, to have four bedrooms and bath upstairs, a large kitchen, dining room, and living room downstairs.

Elizabeth walked into the kitchen to find Rebecca setting seven places at the table and Ronan hunched over the stove in jeans and black T-shirt, cooking what had to be five packages of bacon and four cartons of eggs. An entire loaf of bread, toasted, was piled on a platter, and four more slices popped out of the toaster as she walked in.

Ronan glanced up at her and gave her a wide smile, full of energy. "I do a mean biscuits-and-gravy, but I didn't have time this morning. Scrambled okay with you?"

"Fine."

Rebecca was giving Elizabeth a critical look. "You didn't sleep, did you?"

"Not really."

"Can't blame you."

Rebecca was tall and leggy, but large, nothing willowy about her. She wore jeans and a sleeveless top and had pulled her curly hair into a ponytail. Like Ronan, she had a restless vitality, one that said she might wear human clothes and set the table with matching silverware, but she'd rather be out running through the woods as her bear.

"Sit down, Elizabeth," Ronan said. "We'll fatten you up."

He piled the rest of the bacon and eggs on another platter and carried it and the toast to the table. Elizabeth stared at the mounds of food heading her way.

"A slice of toast is fine with me," she said.

"Best thing for shock is a hearty meal." Ronan stuck his spatula under the eggs and piled a load on her plate. "I've got some roasted red pepper salsa if that's your thing, or good old-fashioned salt and pepper. Butter and jam for the bread, and best of all, honey. Bears like their honey."

Elizabeth wasn't sure whether to laugh or keep it to herself. She settled for a polite thank you. Ronan turned away. "Any time, Lizzie-girl."

Cherie and Olaf appeared as though by magic as Ronan started ladling out the food. Mabel waltzed in a moment later, and Rebecca poured coffee. Mabel sucked down her coffee, closing her eyes in pure enjoyment. Mabel had never been much of an alcohol drinker, thank God, but she worshipped coffee.

"Scott's still in the shower," Cherie said, in universal female derision for males who irritated them.

"I'll talk to him," Ronan said. "Let him be, Cherie. The Transition is hard."

"I'm still getting over mine." Rebecca sat down and shoveled as much food onto her plate as Ronan did onto his. No dieting in this house. "And with more and more males mate-claiming in this Shiftertown, the pickings are getting slim."

"Don't complain, woman," Ronan said. "There's four males for every female around here. It's me, Scott, and Olaf that will be going mateless. You can always hit on Ellison. He's a party animal."

Rebecca snorted. "He's a Lupine who's too full of himself."

Ronan shrugged. "Well, if you're going to be picky."

"What about Spike?" Mabel asked. She scooped up eggs hungrily. "He's cute. All those tatts. And then Connor. Mmm."

"Connor's a cub," Cherie said, wrinkling her nose. "And a Feline. And a Morrissey. And did I mention a *Feline*?"

"What does that mean?" Elizabeth asked as she ate. "A Feline?"

"Means he turns into a wildcat," Cherie answered. "His whole family does. Ellison is a Lupine, a wolf. Wolves are all conceited—think they're noble creatures or something. We're bears, which of course are the best Shifters." She chortled.

"Cool," Mabel said. "Can I see you turn into a bear?"

"No shifting at the table," Ronan growled. "We have company, and I'm not cleaning up the mess."

Cherie winked at Mabel. "Later."

They were going to be BFFs any second, Elizabeth knew it. "We might not have time to do much visiting, Mabel," she said, chewing on thick Texas toast which did taste good with butter and honey. "I have to get back to the store and clean it up before we open. I'm going to need your help. We open at eleven, and it's already eight, so we need to get a move on."

Everyone at the table went quiet. The shower finally snapped off upstairs, adding to the silence.

"Elizabeth, you'll have to keep your store closed today," Ronan said. "I talked to Liam after you went to bed, and he says things are bad for you. So until he and I can work them out, you're staying here."

The entire table was looking at her. Cherie with her mottled hair, Rebecca with her even stare, Olaf with his wide black eyes. Only Mabel kept her gaze on her plate. Elizabeth, who'd learned the dynamics of a group home early in life, realized that as much as Rebecca and the others bantered with him, Ronan was the leader.

Elizabeth pushed back her chair, wiped her mouth on a napkin, and got to her feet. She said to Ronan, "Can we talk outside, please?" and then walked out the back door into the morning heat without waiting to see if he'd follow.

# Chapter Five

Ronan went after her without hesitation. There was nothing better than a cute female with the hottest ass he'd ever seen ordering him around.

Behind him he heard Olaf say, a little fearfully, "Ronan . . . he will punish Lizbeth?"

"No, sweetie," Rebecca said. "But she might punish *him*."

The back door swung shut, cutting off Olaf's reply.

Elizabeth waited by her truck, arms folded. This morning she wore tight blue jeans and a little top that exposed both her navel and the tattoo on her collarbone. It was a butterfly. Nice.

Ronan didn't usually like small women, but decided he'd make an exception for Elizabeth, who was not tall but generously curved. Her smallness made him want to be gentle, although the fire in her eyes said she wasn't about to be gentle with him. Rebecca had that right.

"Let me explain something about the retail business," Elizabeth said as soon as he was within earshot. Human earshot — he could have heard her all the way in the kitchen, and he knew that his family was listening hard. "If your store closes unexpectedly, people think you're not opening again, and they go away and don't come back. I spent years building up this business, and it's the only thing between me and Mabel and the wolf at the door. If I don't open up, I don't make money. In fact, I lose money, because I still have to pay for my inventory and the lease and taxes and everything else. So I'm not letting a full-of-himself kid with a gun stop me. I learned a long time ago that you can't let yourself be a victim — or else you might as well crawl into a hole, block it up behind you, and stay there the rest of your life."

Elizabeth ran out of breath but not fire. Her blue eyes snapped and sparked. Ronan wondered how those eyes would look, blinking sleepily at him from the pillow next to his.

"You done?" he asked.

"I'm not going to argue about this, so don't bother trying. I'm explaining, that's all. I'm very grateful to you and Rebecca for putting us up. I'll give you some cash for the food, but we're out of here."

She tried to walk around Ronan back to the house. Cute. He stepped in front of her.

"Now, let *me* explain, Lizzie-girl," he said. "The kid who robbed you, Julio Marquez, is the brother of the leader of one of the hardest gangs in Houston. He's now moved into Austin to try to take over here, and he's decided that you need to be punished for getting his kid brother arrested. Plus, you're the only witness to the crime, so if you are too dead to testify, so much the better. I'm a witness, but I'm a Shifter, so my testimony doesn't count. Besides, the older Marquez and his crew would have to get to Shiftertown to off me, and they can't. Which is why you're safe here, and why you're staying here until Liam, his trackers, and I make sure they understand that you're off limits. Got it?"

Elizabeth listened with her mouth open, fear at last showing in her eyes. "Are you talking about the Red Avenue gang?"

"I think that's what they're called. You heard of them?"

"I knew a guy whose brother was killed by one of them. Shot while he was walking his little sister home from school, because he owed them money. The leader's name wasn't Marquez, though."

"It is now. According to Sean, he took over not too long ago, and he wants to expand his enterprise. They're into running drugs and guns up out of Mexico. They're like a little army."

Elizabeth's worried look intensified. "Shit."

"So, you aren't going anywhere. Not while these guys are out to get you and your sister."

Ronan watched her battle her fear. She had resilience, he had to give her that. "This is exactly what I mean about not being a victim," she said. "Mabel can stay here—I don't want her getting mixed up in this. But I have to open my store. I have to keep going. If I let a gang close it, I'm done for. They won't attack me in broad daylight, with all the other open stores around, and I can close up early.

That won't be a problem—I don't get as much traffic at night. How's that?"

Ronan started shaking his head and kept on shaking it. "No, sweetie. I'm not taking a chance they won't do a drive-by on you or something. You're staying here."

Now she looked rebellious. The defiant lady who'd streaked her hair and knew how to pick pockets glared at him. "I'm not jeopardizing everything I've worked for to make you feel better."

"It's to keep you safe!"

"How safe am I in a houseful of Shifters? When one won't even get out of the bathroom?"

She wasn't afraid of them, Ronan could tell. Cautious, yes, but not afraid.

"A hell of a lot safer than you are out on the streets."

"But I'm not allowed to leave?" Elizabeth planted her hands on her hips. "There's a saying, that those who give up freedom for safety don't deserve either one. I don't remember who said that—I missed a lot of school as a kid—but it was someone smart."

Ronan lifted his hands. "I get where you're coming from. I really do understand. But damn it, I don't want to see you hurt. I don't want to see them try to burn down your store—with you inside it. When that guy pulled the gun on you last night . . . it seriously pissed me off."

"Well, it seriously pissed me off too. If they try to burn down the store, I can put out the fire faster if I'm there."

"Goddess, woman, I thought she-bears were stubborn."

Elizabeth fixed him with a steely stare. "You ain't seen nothing yet."

Ronan wanted to laugh. Not only was she stubborn but crazy and brave. He knew right then that if he didn't lock her into Rebecca's bedroom, she'd light out for that store as soon as his back was turned. Even if Ronan did lock her in, Elizabeth would find a way out. She was that kind of girl.

"All right." Ronan forced his voice to come down from the frenzied arguing. "We'll do it your way. Partly. Mabel stays here, and you go open your store. I come with you, and we have a couple trackers lurking around outside to keep an eye on things."

Elizabeth's anger didn't diminish. "Shifters lurking around my parking area all day will worry the other shop owners. What if they call the police?"

"No one will see the trackers. They're pretty good at stealth, when they want to be. And Shifters are at your store all the time. You're one of the few who lets us in."

"They come in to *shop*. Not lurk. There's a difference."

"Why don't you ban Shifters? It's your choice."

Elizabeth stopped, annoyed at the change in conversational direction. She obviously didn't like her arguments interrupted. "Because I think laws banning Shifters are stupid. Why shouldn't you be allowed to wear lame T-shirts like everyone else?"

Ronan chuckled. "I'm keeping the Red-Hot Lover one. My point is, because you've been a friend to Shifters, Shifters are happy to look out for you when you need it. I'm putting you under my protection. I already have. All of Shiftertown knows that if anyone wants to mess with you, they mess with me first."

"All of Shiftertown?" Elizabeth regarded him skeptically. "Already knows this? We didn't get here until late last night."

"Liam put the word out."

"At three in the morning?"

Ronan shrugged. "I told you, Felines are nocturnal. By this morning, everyone knew. There's not a Shifter within a hundred miles who'd want to go one-on-one with me, so they'll help you but leave you alone. The Morrisseys outrank me, but that's about it. And they like you too."

"They don't know me."

"You'd be surprised what they know. You are safe here, and so is Mabel. Now, if you're done arguing, let's go open your store."

Ronan started to walk away. He'd learned that the best way to finish an altercation with females was simply to leave. They'd stand there and shout things at your back, but better that than having the argument go on and on and *on*.

"There's one big problem with you going with me," came her voice behind him.

Ronan turned. "What's that?"

Elizabeth had calmed down a little, but her eyes were still alight with determination. "The judge sentenced you to house arrest. You're not supposed to leave Shiftertown at all, except to go to your job."

"Why don't you let me worry about that? Now, are we going?"

"You're not. I get why you want to post the trackers outside my store to keep an eye out. That makes sense. But what happens when a cop comes by and sees you in there with me? Then *I* get arrested too, for aiding and abetting. I can't run my store if I'm in jail."

"I said, let me worry about that."

"Forget it. Stay here and take care of Mabel, and your Spike guy with his tatts can watch out for the gang."

Ronan came back to her. "Here's the deal, Lizzie-girl. I go with you, or you don't go."

"Stop calling me Lizzie-girl." She jabbed her finger at his chest. "It's my store, my life, my sister, and we'll do this my— Hey! What are you doing?"

Ronan had his giant hands on her soft waist, and he lifted her off her feet. She squirmed and glared, but he lifted her higher, higher, until she was over his head. He often picked up Olaf like this, and Elizabeth was not much bigger than the cub.

"Ronan, you put me down!"

"Nothing doing, sweet thing. Not until you realize that I'm your bodyguard now, and that's all there is to that."

"You arrogant . . ."

Ronan saw her hand coming at him, fingers stiff, right for his eyes. He ducked out of the way in time, but the move made him lose his hold. Elizabeth kicked out, not contacting him, but with enough force to twist from his grip and land on her feet. She never touched him, and yet, there she stood, a couple yards from him, hands on hips, breathing hard, triumph on her face.

Ronan growled. "You fight dirty."

"I learned how to a long time ago."

"You know something, Lizzie-girl?"

Elizabeth canted one hip . . . Aw, wasn't that adorable? "What's that?" she asked.

"I fight dirty too."

Before Elizabeth could scream, Ronan ran at her and lifted her again, letting the momentum carry them forward until her back was against the outside wall of the Den. Ronan pinned her tightly, his body against hers, so that she couldn't squirm, kick, or do any neat karate moves with her hands.

Elizabeth struggled, and she glared, and the more she glared, the more Ronan wanted to laugh. She smelled sweet, like the honey she'd poured on her toast. One drop of that honey lingered on the corner of her mouth, and Ronan leaned down and licked it away.

# Chapter Six

Elizabeth froze. She felt the moist heat of his mouth, the flick of his tongue, the warmth of his lips. He was strong, his hands on her waist attested to that, yet his touch on her mouth was everything that was gentle. Elizabeth hung in his grasp for a long moment before she returned the faintest of pressures.

They were face to face, so close that Elizabeth saw the faint line of scar that laced from the corner of his cheekbone up the bridge of his nose. Where he'd broken it, she surmised.

She did nothing. Ronan studied her a long time, his eyes warm, his gaze sliding to her lips.

Slowly Elizabeth brought up one hand to cup his cheek. She let her thumb drift over the firm line of his mouth before she closed the inch between them and kissed him again.

Their lips fused, unmoving heat, slow goodness. Elizabeth felt the thump of his heart, the beat of hers in return, the Texas sunshine soaking into her bones, as hot as her blood.

"Oh, give me a break," came a male voice from the porch. Scott, finally out of the shower and shirtless, leaned on the railing, his dark hair wet. "You told me not to touch the humans, Ronan. Why don't the same rules apply to you?"

Ronan eased out of the kiss. Slowly, he lowered Elizabeth to her feet and turned around.

"I'm taking Elizabeth to her store," Ronan said, voice neither harsh nor conceding. "Mabel is to be protected. She can move around Shiftertown, but not out of it, and one of us is to be with her at all times. Tell Rebecca."

"I'm not a babysitter," Scott growled.

He was defiant, but Elizabeth sensed him backing off under Ronan's stare. Elizabeth had seen these dynamics before, at every home she'd lived in. Sometimes the adult radiated menace and the kid took a step back, shoulders slumping in submission; sometimes it was kid who was in control.

Ronan was definitely in charge here. "Not a babysitter," Ronan said. "A protector. We all are."

"Bodyguards," Elizabeth said. Scott flicked his gaze to her, then took it instantly back to Ronan. "Not my choice, but Ronan's right," Elizabeth went on. "Mabel and I need protection until we figure out how to be safe from these guys. I'd really appreciate it if you made sure Mabel was all right. And if anyone comes looking for her, I'll be glad to know you and Rebecca are around."

Scott's gaze flickered again, but the enraged defiance eased out of him.

"Well, if you're going to stroke my ego, all right then," Scott said. "See, Ronan, you only have to ask nice."

Ronan shrugged. "Elizabeth's nicer than me. Go tell Rebecca, and don't be a shithead."

Scott gave him a sneering look, but it was more mocking than angry. "I'll tell her I found you kissing Elizabeth. I thought you said you'd conquered your mating frenzy a long time ago."

"Go," Ronan growled.

Scott went, but at least now he was laughing.

"I'll be glad when his Transition's done," Ronan said, exasperation in his voice. "It's like living with a volcano."

"What's a mating frenzy?" Elizabeth asked.

"Don't humans have that?"

"No." Elizabeth folded her arms, keeping him out of her space. She shouldn't have let him kiss her, but, damn, she'd enjoyed it.

Ronan moved to his motorcycle and started checking things on it. "Mating frenzy happens at the Transition for the first time, but it can happen any time we scent a potential mate. It *always* happens after a mate-claim is accepted. Mating frenzy means a Shifter wants to mate without stopping, not even to eat. Maybe to sleep, but then only to wake up and mate some more."

"An out-of-control sex drive?" Elizabeth asked. "And you conquered it? I didn't know men *could* conquer their sex drive."

He ignored her attempt at humor. "Once, a long time ago, I almost mated, but she got killed."

Ronan bent to study a dial on his bike, but not before Elizabeth saw the raw pain in his eyes. She went to him. "Ronan, I'm so sorry." She touched his shoulder, strong beneath her hand. "I didn't mean to tease you."

"It's more than fifty years ago now. I've never found anyone I wanted to mate with since."

But it hurt him. Elizabeth saw that. Some hurts never went away, no matter how much you tried.

"Seriously, Ronan, I'm sorry," she said. "That shouldn't have happened to you."

Another shrug. "We need to get to your store."

Elizabeth let it go. She'd also learned that when people didn't want to talk about their pain, they didn't want to talk about their pain.

She started for the pickup, but Ronan shook his head. "Marquez's guys will know your truck. We take my bike."

"What does it matter? They'll know I'm at the store when I get there."

Ronan gave her a look of great patience. "It matters when they're scanning the streets for your truck, and it matters when I need to get you away as fast as I can."

Elizabeth conceded, not so much because she agreed but because she wanted a ride on that bike. Her skin tingled with glee as she headed for it. She'd owned a Harley once upon a time, until some asshole stole it, and she'd never seen it again.

The bike was huge, fitting its large owner. An older model, she saw, but lovingly kept. Ronan handed her a spare helmet. Elizabeth fastened it, then mounted behind him.

The motor throbbed, power between her legs. Elizabeth hung on to Ronan, the man as powerful as the bike, and suppressed a whoop as Ronan tore out of the driveway and onto the street.

*** *** ***

Elizabeth let herself put away her worries to enjoy the ride to the shop. Ronan took it easy, but she felt the bike's energy, its need to open up. What heaven it would be to get this thing out on an empty highway and really let it go.

She felt Ronan's strength as he leaned into the turns, the fluidity of his muscles as he moved with the bike. He knew how to ride, knew how to coax the machine to do what he wanted without fighting it.

"Sweet ride!" she yelled.

The journey ended too soon, Ronan pulling up in the alley behind her store.

All seemed quiet. Ronan let her dismount first and took the helmet from her, but told her to wait for him to scout. "If I tell you to, you get on this bike and go," Ronan said. "I can tell you know how to ride, right?"

Elizabeth nodded. She knew, all right, though this motorcycle would be a challenge, as large as it was.

"Good," Ronan said. "Let me go check it out."

Truth to tell, Elizabeth felt a lot better with Ronan there. If she'd come alone in her pickup this morning, she'd be lingering, debating whether to go inside, and possibly losing the debate. In spite of her brave talk about staying open no matter what, she was afraid.

Watching Ronan walk away wasn't bad, either. He was a big man, but trim, not fat. His ass in those tight jeans was very nice, and the black T-shirt stretching across his shoulders was nice too.

Ronan unlocked the back door of her store and stepped inside. Elizabeth tensed, hands clenching around the motorcycle helmet until she swore she'd dent the plastic. When Ronan came back outside after about fifteen minutes, her entire body relaxed, and she flexed her sore fingers.

"Everything's fine," he said. "No one's in there, the lock hasn't been forced, and I didn't find any booby traps."

"Booby traps?" Elizabeth said, eyes going wide.

"These guys aren't going to fight fair. I checked for tripwires and explosive devices, but I'm pretty sure it's clean."

"*Pretty* sure?"

Ronan actually smiled. "I'll keep looking. Like I said, no one forced the locks or any windows, so I don't think anyone's been inside."

Elizabeth blew out her breath. "All right. Let's go in."

Ronan parked the bike right outside the back door and took the helmets inside with him. The alley door led straight into her office, which was still a mess from the fight the night before. The door to the store hung from its hinges, and the doorframe had splintered where Ronan's big body hadn't quite fit through it.

"I'll get Spike and Ellison over here to fix that," Ronan said. "They're good carpenters."

"I can't pay them much. I only have so much set aside for repairs."

"No paying. I broke the door, I'll get it fixed. Gratis."

Elizabeth rose from picking up papers from the floor. "You mean your friends will come over and replace a door and drywall for free?"

"Sure. We help each other out. Besides, Liam likes you, and if Liam says they do it on the house, they do it on the house."

Elizabeth thought of Liam Morrissey's warm blue eyes and the pressure of his hands when he'd clasped hers. "Are you sure Liam likes me? You were arrested for helping me."

"If Liam didn't like you, you'd know. Trust me."

Yes, she believed that. He'd beamed a charming smile on one and all, but Elizabeth had sensed his controlled power, the dangerous thing beneath his surface.

Elizabeth went through the store, righting things, replacing the displays that had been knocked over. At least Marquez hadn't gotten into the safe. He'd been right that Elizabeth hadn't made her deposit— she'd planned to do it last night, and the safe held several thousand dollars. The police had kept Marquez's shoulder bag full of cash and given her a receipt for a hundred and seventy-eight dollars.

Elizabeth picked up the torn bits of a huge T-shirt and held the strips up before her eyes. Ronan's bear body had ripped its way right out of the shirt. The strength the torn fabric represented made her shiver. She stared at the strips for a time then, for some reason, she rubbed them against her cheek.

A large hand took them away from her. "Throw those out. I trashed that shirt. And I owe you for the other one."

Elizabeth flushed as he tossed the pieces of T-shirt into the wastebasket. "No, no. It's on me. You saved my life and my store. Least I can do. Oh, and, you said you were buying a birthday present last night. For who?"

"Rebecca. Got anything for a horny she-bear who doesn't want to be reminded she's coming up on her hundredth birthday?"

Elizabeth hid her astonishment at the *hundredth* part. "I'll find her something cute. Also on me. You all have been so nice to me."

Ronan nodded, as though it was no big deal, and turned away to answer his cell phone. He continued to make calls after that, she noticed as she kept cleaning.

By the time shoppers had started migrating to the area, and Elizabeth reached to turn on her neon "OPEN" sign—custom-made, with a girl with long legs sitting on the curved end of the *N*—Ronan was off the phone and all was ready.

"The trackers are coming," he said. "Probably they're already here."

"Tell one of them to bring me my phone. If Liam wants it, he can have it, but I need the numbers stored inside."

Ronan rumbled a laugh. "He's done playing. He's sending it."

The cell phone was returned to her via a tall, broad-shouldered Shifter with a shaved head, deep brown eyes, and body art all over him. He gave her a predatory smile as he handed over the phone.

"I'm Spike," he said. "Nice to meet you."

*Spike*. The "hot" guy Mabel said had tatts all over him. He was certainly well inked, his muscle shirt showing art that interlocked and wove up and down his arms like living paintings. His own skin showed only in his face and hands. Like all Shifters, he was tightly muscled and had that edge of animal about him. Elizabeth wondered what he turned into.

Ronan shoved the phone from Spike's side of the counter to Elizabeth's. "You're on perimeter," Ronan growled at him.

Spike shot Ronan a glance, and his evil smile widened. "You're the boss." He walked out of the store without saying good-bye, the small bells on the door tinkling.

"Felines," Ronan said. He might as well have said, *Shitheads*.

"Liam's a Feline," Elizabeth said, tucking her phone into her pocket. "Right?"

"The whole Morrissey clan are Felines. That's why Liam is so full of himself. Like a cat with cream."

"And Spike's a Feline like him?"

"Different clan. Spike's wildcat is bred from jaguars, but the Morrisseys have more lion in them. Spike came up here from Mexico, the Morrisseys from Ireland."

"What do you mean by *more lion*? Aren't they all were-lions or were-jaguars or whatever?"

Ronan shook his head. "We're all Fae-beasts, technically. Feline and Lupine clans tend to lean more toward one cat or wolf type than others, but none of them breed true. Only bears do."

"Of course."

"Bear Shifters were the last ones created. With us, the Fae finally got it right."

"You're saying Bears are the best," Elizabeth said, straight-faced.

"Damn straight."

"And the most modest, obviously."

"Damn straight." He looked so serious when he was full of shit.

"And you're a Kodiak bear, right?" Elizabeth went on. "And Rebecca is too?"

"She's from my clan—a long way removed, but still my clan. It means I can't mate with her, which is fine with me. She's a neat-nik. Drives me frigging insane."

"Then why do you live with her?"

"Not a lot of choice. The humans put me in with Rebecca when I was brought to this Shiftertown. There aren't enough houses to go around, so any family connection means you share. You share even if there's not a family connection, but at least they don't force different species into the same house if they don't want to be there. That would be a blood bath."

No customers had entered the store yet, so Elizabeth allowed herself to lean on her elbows on the counter and keep asking questions.

"And the other three? Mabel said you're basically running a foster home for bears."

"I guess you can put it like that. Cherie came first. She'd been kept in a pen for about ten years, a pen only about five feet square. Some humans up north had caught her as a cub and kept her as a pet. Someone found out, realized what she was, and called the police. The Shifter Division took her, but didn't know what to do with her. I heard about her through Ursines in Wisconsin—their Shiftertown didn't have room for her, so they were asking around. I told Dylan—Liam's dad—about her, and Dylan said we'd bring her down. Poor kid. It took her a long time to adjust to living like a normal Shifter. She still hasn't adjusted, in some ways."

"I'm sorry," Elizabeth said, stunned. Her own childhood had been rough, but nothing like that. "Scott and Olaf have similar stories?"

"Scott came to us because the Shiftertown he was in couldn't handle him. There weren't any other Bears there, only Lupines and Felines. It's hard enough for species to get along, and he went a little crazy being the only Ursine there. So I offered to take him. Scott's not bad, just a pain in the ass. He'll be fine once he finishes his Transition."

"No parents?"

"Father died right before he was born, and his mother died of bringing him in. He's been alone since."

"And Olaf?" Elizabeth bit her lip.

"Saw his mom and dad shot and killed in front of him, but thank the Goddess, he doesn't clearly remember it. Hunters, somewhere up in the Arctic, near Russia. They said they didn't realize the bears were Shifter. Sure. Olaf is cute, so they didn't kill him, but they did try to make a pet of him, like Cherie. Except Olaf nearly killed one of them, so the Russian Shifter Division got him and locked him up for a long time. Again, I got word and said I'd take him. That was a year ago."

Ronan related the tragic tales without changing expression, as though these things were commonplace, which made them all the worse.

"I'm sorry," Elizabeth said again. "That's so wrong."

"At least I have a good Shiftertown leader who lets me help. Some leaders can be real shitheads. I just hope I can help the kids out."

"You already have," Elizabeth said. "I grew up in foster homes, Ronan. I see your house, and it's like paradise. Cherie, Scott, and Olaf are happy there. They can be normal. That doesn't always happen."

Ronan nodded without conceit. "It's funny, when I lived in the wild, I was by myself most of the time. I preferred it. I had miles to roam, didn't have to see anyone if I didn't want to. I never thought I'd be holed up in a house with a prickly she-bear and three cubs, trying to be a substitute dad. But what the hell?"

"From what I can see, you're doing an amazing job."

Ronan pushed himself up from where he'd been leaning on the counter. "Stop flattering me, woman. You're making me blush."

"Fine. But if you're going to hang out here, I have a crate of new stuff that needs to be shelved." She sent him a sweet look. "Since Mabel's not here, you're recruited."

\*\*\* \*\*\* \*\*\*

Pablo Marquez looked across his desk at his little brother Julio, who lounged on the old sofa by the soda machine. Julio's face was bruised and cut from his wrestling match with the bear, and the back of his head still sported bandages.

Pablo had heard that the Bear Shifter had been let go, somehow convincing the judge he'd only been trying to take the gun away from Julio. The problem was, Pablo believed him. If the Shifter had wanted Julio dead, Julio wouldn't be sitting here with only a few shallow cuts as souvenirs.

Julio had been quiet and angry since Pablo had paid his bail and brought him home. He'd had to call in a favor to get Julio out of the hospital and to a bail hearing so quickly.

Now he had a problem. Pablo ran a body shop, a great way to do legitimate business and keep the other businesses under the radar. He was new here in Austin and wanted to keep under the radar from many people for a while. Tough to do that when his little brother decided to go out and do something dumb-ass like try to rob a little novelty shop.

"I want her in the ground," Julio was saying. "That bitch and her trained Shifter."

"You're going to leave her alone," Pablo said sharply. "What the hell did you go in there for? You were going to get, what, maybe two grand, tops?"

Julio shrugged. "I'd get what I'd get."

"What you got was a trial for armed robbery." Pablo balled his hands until the skin pulled against his knuckles. He'd promised their mother he'd look after Julio, even though the kid was a big screw-up. Pablo was fifteen years older than Julio, and he swore that Julio was part of the reason their mother had died of the heart attack.

Pablo had learned on that cruel day that all his money and all his success couldn't keep him from losing the one person in the world he loved. Now he was stuck taking care of Julio and trying to make the best of it.

He continued. "First of all, you didn't scout the place. There was a *Shifter* in there, a big one. The guy has to be seven feet tall, and you never noticed him? *Dios mio,* what do you use for brains?"

"I scouted plenty. I watched that bitch every night for two weeks. I know where she lives and what kind of truck she drives, and what she does after work —

which is nothing—she has a boring life. Shooting her would be doing her a favor. I did everything I was supposed to, Pablo."

"Yeah, well, that Shifter didn't just grow in there. You are telling me you never saw him walk in?"

"No. I bet he was there in her back room before I got there. I bet she was fucking him. I bet she gets off fucking Shifters in her office."

Pablo held on to his patience with effort. Julio liked the *F*-word and enjoyed opportunities to use it.

"So what if she does?" Pablo asked. "The point is, he was there, and you didn't know it. It would have been justified if he'd killed you."

Julio looked offended. "What are you saying?"

"I'm saying you screwed up. You decided to pull a smalltime job and then you messed it up by being careless. You're an idiot."

"I want that bitch to pay!"

"And she will. But my way. I'm trying not to draw attention to myself, and you are very definitely drawing attention. Killing her obviously will only make it worse, so don't even think about trying it."

Julio looked pensive. "What do you mean, killing her *obviously*?"

"A drive-by, an execution, even a car accident— anything suspicious will point back to you, and then I'll be up to my ass in cops. I don't want to be up to my ass in cops. Understand?" Pablo stopped at Julio's guilty expression. "Why? What have you done now?"

Julio's voice was so quiet Pablo had to strain to hear him. "I sent Menendez and his brother to wait for her and follow her home."

Pablo rose, fists on his desk. "You know, Julio, if anyone else in my crew acted like you, I'd lose them. You get away with this shit because you're my brother, and I promised Mamita I'd take care of you. Get on your phone and call them back."

"What the fuck? Damn it, Pablo, if you override my order, I'll never have any cred."

"*Cred*. You watch too many movies. Get them back here, *now*. I can still bust your ass, and I'll do it."

Julio said a few dark things, but he took out his cell phone.

Pablo sat back down and started making calls of his own. He needed to do something about the woman with the store, because she was a witness against Julio, and Pablo couldn't afford to have his brother going to prison right now. He'd put the bitch in her place, but he'd do it more subtly than Julio ever could. As for the Shifter — well, Pablo knew how to take care of Shifters. The Shifter would be the least of their problems.

He ignored his sulky little brother, gathered the reins of his power, and went to work.

# Chapter Seven

Spike came back in to report around three. Ronan talked to him alone in the office, Elizabeth busy out front. She had expressed concern that people would stay away when they found out there'd been an attempted robbery at her store, but apparently, curiosity was a greater motivator than fear.

"Saw a car with two guys," Spike said. "They went by a couple of times, slowing down to watch the shop. Fourth time they went by, one of the guys was on the phone, then all the sudden, they take off. Haven't seen them since."

"Did they see you?" Ronan asked.

"No one sees me if I don't want them to."

"Anything else?" Ronan asked.

"No, just those guys. I'll keep an eye out for them."

"Thanks."

Spike shrugged. "Hey, it's my job." He went out the back door to the alley, his movements spare and quiet.

Ronan watched from the office doorway as Elizabeth went about her business. She was a natural at selling, he decided. He watched her greet her customers, talking to them in a friendly way without getting too personal. This was a novelty store, which meant she sold everything from T-shirts with funny logos to plastic handcuffs. Nothing distasteful, just fun stuff that people mostly bought as gifts for friends. The customers tended to be upbeat, laughing with each other over the zany thing they'd give whoever for a birthday, retirement, anniversary, bridal shower, bachelor party.

Elizabeth had a way of putting people at their ease, helping them find exactly the right thing. Ronan saw, though, that she maintained a distance. That made sense while she sold things to perfect strangers, but he'd noticed it at the house too. Elizabeth didn't let anyone get too close. She was friendly, yes, but any personal question was deftly turned aside or evaded.

Ronan had asked Sean to run her name in the database. Sean had access to a vast network, built by Guardians over the last two decades, which contained more information than any non-Shifter could possibly imagine. Humans didn't know about this network, which ran on a lot of technical know-how coupled with a little bit of magic. Only Guardians knew how to access it, and only Guardians were allowed to use it—Guardians being those Shifters who stuck their swords into the bodies of dead or near-dead Shifters to send their souls to the afterlife.

Sean had run Elizabeth's name but turned up nothing. She had no police record, not even a minor traffic ticket, and neither did Mabel. Elizabeth was thirty, according to her driver's license, and had lived in Austin for about six years, owning the store called SoCo Novelties for five. She'd bought the business as a whole from the previous owner who'd retired.

Ronan thought about how she'd skillfully plucked Kim's card from his pocket, and wondered again. Elizabeth Chapman had picked pockets before, and she fought like a street kid. Juvenile records were sealed, sure, but not to the Guardians. They could hack anything.

Sean had added the little detail that there was no record of Elizabeth at all before her move to Austin. A reference to an address in El Paso when she'd rented an apartment upon her arrival in Austin, but that El Paso address turned out to be bogus. She'd used her store as proof of residence or proof of income for everything else, including the small house she'd purchased a few years ago. She paid all her taxes, no under-the-table dealings, and had a social security number, bank accounts, and IRAs for herself and Mabel.

So who had Elizabeth Chapman been before she'd become Elizabeth Chapman? And why had she needed to turn into someone else?

The store did brisk business, but Elizabeth closed down at eight when the crowd started to thin. People still wandered the streets to seek restaurants or to walk down to the bridge to watch the bats emerge, but all but the most dedicated shoppers departed. Elizabeth turned off her sign and locked up.

"I'm making this deposit tonight," she said, heading toward the office. "You've been here all day, Ronan. Don't you have a job of your own?"

"Starts at nine," Ronan said. "I'll take you to the bank on my way."

"You go. Spike can drive me. I don't want you to be late because of me. You've already done so much."

Ronan stepped squarely in front of her. "Spike drives like a maniac, and he's heading the same place I am. You're stuck with me, sweetheart."

"What place?" Elizabeth caught up her lock bag and turned out the lights. "Where do you work, anyway?"

"Shifter bar." He opened the back door for her but walked outside first, as Shifters did, to check that the way was safe. "I'm the bouncer. Come and say hi to everyone."

*** *** ***

Ronan took her on his motorcycle to the bank around the corner and stood close guard—at the same time keeping himself out of sight of bank cameras—while Elizabeth put the deposits into the slot. After that, she was free.

As Ronan pulled out onto Congress and headed for the bridge and downtown, Elizabeth again felt the heady joy of simply riding with him. She wished they could go on through the city and keep on riding, to the long, empty stretches of highway Texas had so much of. Out there, in the darkness, they could find freedom.

But Ronan had people to take care of, as did she. Responsibility was a tether, but at least in Elizabeth's case, it was a tether of love. She thought, as they sped toward the illuminated dome of the capitol building and the Saturday night craziness of Sixth Street, that the tether Ronan had found here had become one of affection, even if it hadn't started that way.

Ronan drove through downtown and out again into darkness and more derelict streets. He pulled up in front of a bar near the open field that led to Shiftertown. The bar was a squat, dark building with no windows and a small parking lot already filled with people. No, not people . . . Shifters.

There were plenty of humans in the mix too, Elizabeth saw as they dismounted and walked to the bar. Shifter groupies, mostly, she saw—humans of both sexes who liked to hang out with Shifters, some wearing fake Collars. More than one woman looked at Ronan with appreciation and calculation, which irritated Elizabeth for some reason.

The bar inside was crowded, with tunes playing on a jukebox and Shifter waitresses hurrying back and forth to serve beers and take away empties. The bartender was human, Elizabeth saw. Maybe Shifters weren't allowed to actually dispense the drinks. Liam Morrissey didn't own this bar, she knew—a human did. Shifters couldn't own property, but Liam could work for the human owner and manage the place.

A number of Shifters greeted Ronan by name or slapped hands with him as he went by. Interestingly, many greeted Elizabeth by name, including the six-foot blonde called Glory who was a regular at

Elizabeth's store, but they were deferential, looking to Ronan first.

Ronan led Elizabeth through the crowd, staying close by her side. Some of the groupies looked at her with envy, some with resentment.

Kim Fraser came forward to meet her. She opened her arms to Elizabeth and gave her a hug with a squeeze. "I'm glad you came. Let's go into the office."

Elizabeth threw a glance to Ronan, who shook his head. "What's up?" Ronan rumbled.

"Nothing terrible. Liam just wants a word."

Elizabeth stopped. "I want to call Mabel. We like to check in with each other."

"Mabel's here." Kim pointed across the bar to where Mabel sat in a booth with the lanky Connor Morrissey, Scott, and a dark-haired Shifter woman who was obviously pregnant. The dark-haired woman gave Kim a nod, said something to Mabel, and pointed. Mabel looked around and sent Elizabeth a cheerful wave.

"Andrea will take care of her," Kim said. "Mabel was getting antsy, cooped up at Ronan's, so Liam said it was all right if she came. Don't worry. She's in good hands."

Elizabeth was going to have to have a talk with Mabel. Mabel was of legal age, so that wasn't a problem, but she looked way too cozy laughing and talking with the Shifters. Mabel was very accepting of people as they were, something Elizabeth had always admired about her, but then, Mabel wasn't the greatest judge of character, either.

Or maybe Elizabeth was being too protective. She'd always gone back and forth about Mabel, torn between wanting to shield her from the evils of the world and fearing to stifle her with too much restriction.

Kim guided Elizabeth to a door marked "Private," and Ronan came so close behind her that Elizabeth felt his body heat.

On the other side of the door she found Liam Morrissey inside a cluttered office. Liam sat behind a desk, his long legs propped on the desk's top, and he held a baby on his lap.

Elizabeth wasn't sure which was more incongruous—the child held up by Liam's big hands or the man standing on the other side of the room with a huge sword strapped to his back, the hilt slanting above his head.

"He's underage," Elizabeth said, looking at the baby.

"*She*," Liam said. "Katriona Sinead Niamh Morrissey. Sinead for her auntie, Niamh for her grandmum, and Katriona because we like it. Born three months ago."

"And you'd think she was queen of the gods," Ronan said. "The attention she gets." Ronan went around Elizabeth to the baby and gently poked her stomach.

"Shifter?" Elizabeth asked.

Kim reached for the child. At the same time her hands closed around Katriona's waist, Liam leaned up to Kim and kissed her on the lips. It was a warm, loving kiss, the look in Liam's eyes heart-melting.

Elizabeth's thoughts flashed back to Ronan licking the corner of her mouth earlier this morning. His lips had been smooth and warm, soothing. And arousing.

She swallowed and made herself not look at Ronan as Kim snuggled Katriona under her chin.

"I can't wait to see what her wildcat looks like," Kim said. "We won't know for a few years. Shifter-human cubs are born human and then shift when they're about three. Pure Shifter cubs do it the opposite."

Kim bounced Katriona as she talked, Katriona looking at everyone with round blue eyes, while trying to stuff her entire fist into her mouth. Kim moved across the room to the swordsman, who relaxed his grim stance to touch the baby's nose.

Ronan was the only one not at ease. "What do you want, Liam? Elizabeth's had a long day. I brought her here because I thought she could relax a little and then go home."

"She will." Liam retained his nonchalant pose, feet on the desk, hands now laced behind his head. He was watchful, alert while pretending not to be.

Ronan took a step closer to Elizabeth, and she felt the tight muscles of his arm brush her shoulder. "What do you want, Liam?" he repeated, an edge to his voice.

"Just a chat. First, to tell Elizabeth that we're grateful to her testimony that kept you out of jail." Liam gave her a nod. "It was brave of you to stand up for him."

"It was brave of Ronan to rush a guy with a pistol," Elizabeth said. "I couldn't let him take the fall for that."

"But so many humans would." Liam's gaze held no hostility, but at the same time, his blue eyes fixed on her, catching her like a fly in a web so finely spun it was undetectable until too late.

"You're unique, Ms. Chapman," Liam said. "So unique that I can't find out anything about you. Not one single scrap of information. Correction—*Sean* can't find out anything about you, and Sean is a master at it." He glanced at the swordsman across the room who said nothing.

Elizabeth's mouth went dry, and she felt control of her life washing away like a branch caught in a flash flood. She'd thought herself safe—she was supposed to be safe. *No one will ever be able to crack this*, her friend had told her, and she'd paid good money for him to make sure it never happened.

"But you know all about me," she said, forcing her voice to remain steady. "I own SoCo Novelties, I'm Mabel's sister, and I don't mind Shifters coming into my store. That's all there is to know."

Liam's voice remained soft, but he had no need to shout to let her know he held the authority in this room. "You see, Elizabeth, it's my job as Shiftertown leader to protect my Shifters. You were great to help Ronan, and I'm happy that you did. But Ronan's putting himself on the line to take care of you, and that's a big risk to him. A risk to him is a risk to me and to all the Shifters living in his house. Maybe your secrets are innocent ones; maybe they represent no danger." Liam's feet came down, and he rose, tall and intimidating, his charm gone. "But maybe they do. So I need you to tell me the truth, Elizabeth Chapman, before I let you out of here. Who exactly are you?"

# Chapter Eight

Ronan scented the sharp spice of Elizabeth's fear. He also scented her defiance, even before she spoke.

"That's really none of your business, Liam," she said clearly.

Liam's eyes widened, and despite Ronan's disquiet, he wanted to laugh. The arrogant Feline had grown used to people obeying him without question. *People* meaning everyone but his wife, his brother, father, and nephew. All other Shifters pretty much fell in line.

"When you're in Shiftertown, you're under my jurisdiction," Liam said. "It is my business."

"We're not in Shiftertown right now." Elizabeth took a step forward. She was afraid to, Ronan knew, but she did it anyway. "My past has nothing to do with Shifters, and it's nothing that can hurt Shifters."

"Will you let me be the judge of that?" Liam asked.

"No. I said it's none of your business."

"Lass." Liam's voice gentled, which meant he was falling back on the coaxing approach. "I have one of my very best fighters guarding you. I want to know who he's guarding. I can't chance endangering him. Neither can his family."

"I never said he had to guard me," Elizabeth said. "If you don't want me endangering Shifters, then Mabel and I are happy to leave Shiftertown."

She started to turn away. Ronan stopped her by simply not moving. "You're not going anywhere until the threat to you has been eliminated."

Elizabeth's eyes flickered at the word *eliminated*. "If Liam won't be happy until he hears all my secrets, then I can't stay," she said. "He'll have to be disappointed."

"Lass," Liam began, again in the coaxing tone.

"Leave her alone, Liam," Ronan said. He looked at Elizabeth and her blue eyes, not at Liam. "She doesn't want to tell you."

"Ronan, she's using a false name. Until six years ago, she didn't exist."

"She exists now."

"Ronan . . ."

"I said, *leave her alone, Liam.*"

The room went quiet. Ronan expected Sean to come charging across to stand by his brother, his sword a silent threat. He'd seen them do that, and Shifters wilt under the double-alpha stare.

Sean didn't move or speak. Neither did Kim, who usually was ready with some opinion. Even baby Katriona made no noise.

"Do you want to make that official?" Liam said in a quiet voice. "Be responsible for her?"

"Vouch for her, you mean?" Ronan let Liam hold his gaze. He'd already vouched for Scott, Cherie, and Olaf—clan-less, family-less Shifters with bad pasts. No one knew what the cubs would do or what kind of adults they'd become. Ronan had vowed with his life that they'd not be threats. Liam was asking him to do the same for Elizabeth.

"No," Ronan said.

Liam's eyes went wider, and Kim stirred. "Liam, stop it. You too, Ronan. This is Elizabeth's choice. She's not a cub. She's not even Shifter. The same rules don't apply."

"Much as I hate disagreeing with you, love, they do," Liam said. "Will you let him vouch for you, Elizabeth? That means that, if you are lying to us, or you put a foot wrong, it's on his head."

"No!" Elizabeth said fiercely. "What is wrong with you all? I didn't ask you to bring us to Shiftertown. I'm grateful for your help, but I don't have to stay with you. So thank you, but I'm leaving."

Again Ronan stopped her by being too big for her to walk around. "I said I wouldn't vouch for you," he said. "But that's because I'm going to go one better, and mate-claim you."

"Ronan," Liam said, warning in his voice.

"Mate-claim?" Elizabeth said. She took a step back, which put her against Liam's desk. "What does that mean?"

"It means not only do I vouch for you, but I ensure that all Shifters stay away from you, always, including Liam. The bond of the mate supersedes the authority of the clan leader and even the Shiftertown leader. If Liam has a problem with you, he has to come through me first. Trust me, he doesn't want to have to go through me."

Liam, instead of getting upset, sat down and leaned back in his chair again, grinning his annoying Irish grin. "It's an interesting solution," he said. "Very interesting."

Elizabeth looked from Liam to Ronan. "What are you saying? That I'm now your mate? I don't want a mate!"

"Tell her she can reject the claim," Kim said. "Be fair. She doesn't understand complicated Shifter rules."

Liam shrugged. "A mate-claim only means that Ronan now protects you, and that you're off-limits to all other Shifter males. Doesn't mean you're mated. Yet. And yes, you can reject the claim. He can't force it on you." Liam said the last part reluctantly, as though he'd be happy for Elizabeth to be stuck in the claim.

"Then I reject—"

Ronan put his fingers over Elizabeth's mouth. "Wait. Let it work, first. If you stay under my claim, then Liam can't make you tell him about your past, or any other detail he wants to poke his nose into. I stay with you and protect you from angry gang leaders who want to kill you. Once the danger is over, you can reject the claim. We can't stop you. That's Shifter law."

"I'm not Shifter," Elizabeth said, her breath warm on his fingers.

"Doesn't matter. I am. Elizabeth Chapman, I mate-claim you, witnessed by Liam the leader of the Austin Shiftertown, Sean the Guardian, Kim the leader's mate, and Katriona, the leader's firstborn."

As Elizabeth stared at him over his blunt fingers, Ronan sensed a *click* inside himself, as though something that had long been unresolved had at last completed.

Elizabeth was a survivor. Ronan saw that in her. She was a survivor as much as he was, as much as the cubs in his house were, as much as Liam and his family were.

Elizabeth drew a breath. "All right. For now, I won't reject it."

Ronan relaxed, feeling a tightness in him loosen and flow away. Elizabeth held his gaze, her chin lifted. Nothing submissive about her.

"But that doesn't mean I'll do everything you say," Elizabeth said.

Ronan growled, feeling suddenly playful. Wait until he got her home and she looked at him with that challenge in her eyes. He'd never mate-claimed anyone before. Was this how it felt, an unexpected lightness, sudden joy? An excitement, anticipation of the next moment, of every moment? Ronan no longer wanted to work his shift. He wanted to take Elizabeth home and simply *be* with her.

Liam looked past Ronan to his brother. "Sean? You've not said a word. What do you think?"

Sean came out of his relaxed stance, unstrapped his sword, and tossed it to the battered sofa. "I'm thinking you brought me back here, away from my mate, for nothing," he said, moving to the door. "Elizabeth knows what she's doing, and you don't need me."

Without another word, the quiet Morrissey opened the door wide and walked out into the noise. Ronan watched him make straight for Andrea, and

Andrea smile up at him in her warm way, welcoming him back.

*** *** ***

Elizabeth sensed the change in Ronan as he led her out of the office again. He guided her with his hand on the small of her back, gentle pressure, but one she couldn't ignore.

She noticed that every Shifter outside the office looked at Elizabeth in open curiosity as they emerged, then they glanced at Ronan, then again at Elizabeth, then their expressions blanked, and they looked away or backed off. They did it subtly, pretending they didn't, but they did it. How they knew Ronan had made this "mate-claim," Elizabeth didn't know, but it didn't matter. They knew.

Sean was now sitting in the booth with Mabel and the dark-haired, pregnant woman, and Elizabeth headed that way, Ronan tightly beside her. Scott had vacated one place, though Mabel and Connor remained, sitting firmly together.

Before Elizabeth and Ronan made it across the floor, a tall, blond man in cowboy boots and a button-down shirt, sleeves rolled up to expose brawny forearms, walked right in front of them, longneck in hand. The jukebox had started up with a country tune that was part gritty rock.

"Hey, there," the Shifter said. "I'm Ellison, and I need someone to dance with. Someone female. That lets you out, Ronan."

He hadn't looked at Ronan, keeping Elizabeth pinned with his gaze. His gray eyes held the predatory tinge of a wolf's.

Elizabeth shrugged, feeling itchy. The music had a good beat, and she liked the song. "Sure, I'd love to."

Ellison started to reach for her, then he inhaled sharply and looked at Ronan. Ronan never moved, never said a word, but Ellison's face fell. "Aw, hell, Ronan. Why does every pretty woman who comes near Shiftertown get grabbed before I even meet her? You all could save one for me."

"You snooze, you lose," Ronan said.

"You can reject it, you know," Ellison said to Elizabeth. "The mate-claim."

"So I've been told." Elizabeth was suddenly fed up with everything. She'd been anxious about Mabel and about her store, which one of Marquez's men could be torching even at this moment. Now she had to add Shifters, mate-claims, and macho males who passed females around like pieces of meat. All right, so maybe the last thought was unjust, but they seemed to regard women as things to protect from each other and the rest of the world.

Elizabeth straightened her shoulders. "I said I'd dance. Don't you have to work or something, Ronan?"

If she thought Ellison would laugh and waltz away with her, she was wrong. Ellison kept his gaze on Ronan. "Do you mind?" he asked. "Promise I won't touch."

Ronan considered a moment, then he nodded. "Take care of her."

"Hot damn. Come on. Before the song's over."

Ellison led Elizabeth off but carefully didn't touch her until they reached the dance floor. Elizabeth looked over her shoulder at Ronan, who watched them go, unmoving. Ronan stared at them for a while, then he turned his broad back and made for the entrance of the club, where he stationed himself like a sentinel.

Ellison could dance. He had a long-legged grace despite his large size, and could two-step with the best of them. He never lost the beat and led Elizabeth so she didn't, either. He twirled her and spun with her, all with great enjoyment. Through it all, she never lost her awareness of Ronan. The entire club separated her from Ronan, but Elizabeth sensed him at the door, solid as a boulder, his big arms folded, his gaze taking in everything.

When the song ended, another similar one began, and Elizabeth readily kept dancing.

"Are you the Ellison that Ronan said he'd have help me with some carpentry?" she yelled over the music.

"Yep," Ellison said. "Spike and me will come by tomorrow. You close up on Sundays, right?"

She did, but Elizabeth usually went in to catch up on paperwork, ordering, inventory, accounts, and everything else. "Tell me something," she said. "Why is everyone acting like Ronan owns me?"

"He does, if he mate-claimed you. It's hands off for all other Shifters."

"To keep me safe, I thought," Elizabeth said. "Not to dictate every move I make."

Ellison stepped in close. "Honey, we're Shifters. It means we're horn-dogs most of the time. The minute you walked in here, every unmated male — which is most of them — wanted to howl. But now that Ronan's claimed you, we know we have to back off. When you reject the claim, though, you'll be fair game again, and we can go back to being rabid males after you. Rivals with each other instead of friends. Until someone else beats us to the claim."

"Are you serious?"

"Damn right I am."

The dance had them part again, and Elizabeth pondered what he'd said. She'd spent her life struggling to remain independent, to keep from having to rely on a man for . . . well, for anything. She'd watched girlfriends become victims to abusive men they were certain they couldn't live without. *If I leave him, who takes care of me?* they'd ask.

Elizabeth had learned to take care of herself. So much so that when she'd had to cut her losses and run, she'd been able to do it. If she hadn't run, her life would have become pure hell, and she shuddered to think what Mabel's life would have been. Much of her decision had been for Mabel's sake.

Now she'd walked into a society where the males thought nothing of saying openly, *That woman is mine. Hands off.* Animals in mating season fought each other, sometimes to the death, and Shifters had a lot of animal in them.

She glanced over at Sean and Andrea. They were sitting alone in the booth now, Mabel and Connor dancing together not far away. Sean sat against the wall, Andrea leaning back against him in the circle of his arms, and he had his hand on her abdomen, where his child slept. Protective, yes, but also loving. One didn't always go with the other, in Elizabeth's experience.

She thought of Liam and Kim, with their closeness, so comfortable, and Liam holding Katriona on his lap with a look of open love. Perhaps these

Shifters had discovered something that had eluded Elizabeth all her life.

Elizabeth looked at Ronan, who was standing at the door, watching people go in and out. He caught her eye and sent her, not a smile, but a reassuring nod.

A little warmth wound through her heart. Elizabeth would make him pay a bit for so obviously giving her his "permission" to dance with Ellison, but it was nice to think that Ronan was there for her. If she was going to have anyone stand up for her, Ronan was a good person to do it.

Meanwhile, she had fun dancing with Ellison. For the first time since the robbery, Elizabeth relaxed. She realized that no one was going to come into this bar and threaten her or try to kill her, not with Ronan on guard and this many Shifters in here. Marquez or whoever he sent wouldn't make it a step inside the door.

Strange to think that in a Shifter bar right outside of Shiftertown, she was safe. She decided to enjoy the feeling while she had it.

The bar closed at two, but when Elizabeth finally stopped dancing at midnight and sat down, she was exhausted.

"Mabel, let's go home. I mean, to Ronan's house."

Mabel looked at her in surprise across the table. "Are you kidding me? The night is young."

Mabel, at least, was good about not drinking too much. She enjoyed a beer or two, but she liked talking to people and dancing more.

"You lazed around all day," Elizabeth said. "I need some sleep."

"Go, then. Connor or Liam will get me home. Or Glory."

Mabel had adapted to Shiftertown quickly. But then, Mabel had always liked Shifters.

In the end, Andrea and Sean walked Elizabeth home. When Elizabeth said good night to Ronan on the way out, he stopped her and drew her into his arms for a big hug.

Ronan's arms were strong and lifted Elizabeth off her feet, but as he'd been at the house earlier that morning, he was as gentle as gentle could be. Elizabeth found herself looking into his big face, at his scarred nose and his warm brown eyes. She felt not only safe in his arms, but *right*. As though she belonged there.

He touched a kiss to her lips—brief and tender, almost chaste, but the spark behind it held heat.

"I'll be home soon, Lizzie-girl," he said.

"Good," was all Elizabeth could think to say.

Ronan set her down and gave her another brief kiss. "Go on, now."

Sean and Andrea waited a discreet distance away. When Elizabeth caught up to them, she saw that both of them looked amused.

"Is something funny?" Elizabeth asked, annoyed.

They started walking through the field that led to Shiftertown. "No," Andrea said. She was a wolf Shifter, Ellison had told her—like Ellison himself. A Lupine. She had gray eyes, as Ellison did. She was very pregnant, but she walked swiftly and strongly, as though she barely noticed her condition. "Ronan's a good friend."

"And a good man," Sean said, his Irish lilt like music in the night. "He's done me many a good turn. Now he's doing you one."

Elizabeth nodded. "I know he is."

Sean merely looked at her, his eyes speaking volumes.

"Wait a minute," Elizabeth said in amazement. "Are you worried that *I'll* hurt *Ronan*? Well, you don't need to be. He's helping me out, and I'm grateful. When this is over, I'll pay him back. That's all."

"That's not what I'm seeing," Sean said. Moonlight shone on his sword, a weapon, but one of great beauty. "I'm seeing a lonely Shifter looking at a woman like he might have a chance at some happiness. If you're not looking like that back at him, tell him now. Put him out of his misery."

"I only met him last night," Elizabeth said. "Give us a break."

Andrea said, "It can happen fast. You look at each other, and you *know*." She rested her hand on her abdomen and shot a look at Sean. He caught it. A lover's look, exchanging secrets without exchanging words.

"You two need to be alone?" Elizabeth joked. "Seriously. I like Ronan. I have no plans to hurt him. I might not be able to have a relationship with him, but I won't hurt him. I promise you that. I like him too much."

Sean's eyes glittered. "Why can't you?"

"Why can't I what? Have a relationship with him, you mean?" Elizabeth shrugged, her shoulders tight. "I don't know. Things don't always work out. I haven't been very good at relationships in the past. In fact, I suck at them."

"You hold people at arm's length," Sean said. "Don't look surprised, lass. I see you doing it. Even with your sister. But I'm glad to not hear you say, *Because he's Shifter.*"

"He being a Shifter makes it more of a challenge," Elizabeth said. "But obviously, it can be done. Liam and Kim. Ellison says the waitress Annie is going out with a human. And all those groupies sure want it to happen."

"So, why not, then?" Sean asked. "Everyone's bad at relationships until you find the relationship worth fighting for. Or maybe you're already married? Is that the big secret you don't want to tell Liam?"

"What? No," Elizabeth said forcefully. "No, I never married anyone. That I can promise."

"Then what?"

"Sean," Andrea broke in. "Leave the poor woman alone. Not every female has to fall for the hot, sexy, alpha-male Shifter."

Sean blinked. "Why not? I thought we were irresistible."

"You're a comedian, Sean Morrissey," Andrea said.

Sean dropped the subject, and Elizabeth walked without speaking after that, enjoying the banter between the other two. She'd never had that kind of bantering fun with a man—except, she realized, with Ronan.

Sean and Andrea walked her all the way to Ronan's house, where Elizabeth said good night. She had to say good night the Shifter way, she realized, when Andrea gave her a warm, cushy hug, and Sean caught her around the shoulders one-armed and pulled Elizabeth hard against him.

Andrea didn't seem to think it unusual that her mate hugged another woman. They walked off together, very close, but not touching—alert to fight if necessary?

Rebecca was still up and told Elizabeth cheerfully that there was supper hot in the kitchen. Elizabeth found a gigantic soup pot half full of thick beef and barley soup, a huge loaf of bread, and jars of five different flavors of jam to go with the bread.

Hungry, Elizabeth ladled soup into a bowl and threw a piece of bread on top of it. "How does Ronan afford to feed all of you on a bouncer's paycheck?"

Rebecca gave her a nonchalant shrug. "I guess we're good shoppers."

"Sorry," Elizabeth said quickly. "It's none of my business."

"No worries." Rebecca caught up a large purse. "Speaking of that, I need to go out. Will you watch Olaf for me? He's usually asleep by now, but he's a little keyed up because you and Mabel are staying here. He likes company. Cherie's spending the night with a friend, and I don't want to leave him alone."

"Sure," Elizabeth said readily.

Rebecca hesitated. "If you'd rather not, I can wait for Ronan."

Elizabeth took a bite of soup and found it delicious. "No, no. That's fine. I like Olaf. You go . . . shop." *When all the stores are closed. Hmm.*

"Thanks." Rebecca breezed out, banging the door behind her.

Olaf was in the living room watching television. The TV was an old model—no flat screens or HD for

Shifters. A rerun of a seventies comedy was playing. Olaf wasn't so much watching it as standing in front of the screen, staring at the people on it as though trying to figure out what on earth they were doing.

"I like this one," Elizabeth said. "One of the ladies I lived with when I was little loved this show. She was nice." In retrospect Elizabeth knew she should have been kinder to the woman, but Elizabeth had been so afraid of being split up from Mabel that she'd been prickly and defensive. The sweet old lady had understood that, Elizabeth saw now.

Olaf listened as though Elizabeth imparted great wisdom, then he abandoned the television and climbed up onto the sofa beside her. Olaf was nine, Ronan had said, but he acted younger. Maybe because Shifters matured at a much slower rate than humans, or maybe because Olaf had been through a lot.

As Olaf seated himself against Elizabeth, she noted that his white-blond hair bore tiny blue streaks. *Mabel.*

Elizabeth was tired, but she was happy to eat the terrific soup and have the warmth of Olaf beside her. This reminded her of what she and Mabel would do in the bad old days, sitting tightly side-by-side as though that would keep them together forever. *I won't ever let us be split up, Mabel. I promise.*

She'd kept her promise, no matter what.

When the show ended, and Elizabeth set down her empty bowl, Olaf climbed down from the sofa, calmly removed his clothes, and shifted. He did it too close to the coffee table, which got shoved over, but Elizabeth found herself looking at the cutest polar bear cub she'd ever seen.

Not that she'd seen many, not *this* close. Olaf made a little baby growl then climbed back onto the sofa, his long claws tearing the fabric. He flopped down next to Elizabeth, put his head and one paw on Elizabeth's lap, and closed his eyes.

Elizabeth went still, the trust Olaf was showing both stunning and warming her.

Olaf stirred a little, then let out his breath, eyes closing more tightly. Elizabeth couldn't stop herself from stroking his fur. She found it both soft and strong, sort of wiry without being tough.

Elizabeth went on petting him, finding comfort in the act. Olaf's breath whuffed hot over her blue-jeaned knee, the cub relaxing into sleep.

Rebecca didn't return. Elizabeth lifted the remote and switched off the television, and silence crept over the house. They didn't have any clocks in here, so nothing ticked. There was only the quiet of the outside world, the faint breeze through the open window. Austin summers were hot and sticky, but the coming fall could be cool and clean.

She was still sitting there, Olaf half on her lap, when Ronan came in.

# Chapter Nine

Again Elizabeth was struck with how *quiet* he was. When he'd charged Marquez in her store, she hadn't heard a thing until he'd reached them.

Ronan saw Olaf sleeping, closed his mouth on the greeting he'd been about to give her, and stepped inside. A cool breeze stirred wind chimes on the porch and wafted through the windows.

"Where's Mabel?" Elizabeth whispered.

"With Cherie. I took her to Cherie's friend's. Two doors down."

"Connor?"

Ronan righted the coffee table, which had been left on its side, and put her empty bowl back on it. Nothing had broken, at least. "Took him home. Scott's staying over at the Morrisseys tonight too, so it will be less crowded here. Becks went out?"

"She implied shopping, but nothing's open this late."

"Means she's prowling. Becks is past ready to mate, but she's being very picky."

"What about Ellison? He seems like he'd be willing."

Ronan grimaced. "Goddess, I hope not. He's a Lupine. That's all I'd need, half-wolf, half-bear Shifters all over the place, full of themselves, like Ellison."

"How would that work?" Elizabeth remained still as Ronan collapsed on the sofa next to her, stretching into a sprawl. Olaf never moved. "How can a Shifter be half wolf, half bear?"

"Wouldn't. The cubs would be born in human shape and then take their animal form a few years later. They'll go one way or the other, so a Lupine-Ursine mating could have half the family wolves and half bears. That would be interesting."

Elizabeth gave Olaf another soft stroke. "Olaf's already big. What's going to happen when he's fully grown? Polar bears are gigantic."

"And Shifter polar bears are even bigger." Ronan stretched his arm across the back of the sofa, touching her shoulders. "We'll deal with that when we need to. Rebecca and Cherie might be mated and gone by the time he reaches full size. I built the Den to be plenty big."

"For Olaf?"

"Built it before he came. But sure."

"None of this fazes you."

Ronan cupped Elizabeth's shoulder with his big hand. He smelled like the night overlaid with the warmth of himself. "None of what?"

"Having cubs live in your house. Saving me from being shot. Having me and Mabel move in. Mate-claiming me so Liam would stop asking me questions."

He moved with his shrug. "I take things as they come."

"Most people don't. Most people stress out. I know I do."

Ronan regarded her with calm, dark eyes. "I lived a long time alone. You learn to take life slowly when you live like that. Why worry about what terrible thing will happen tomorrow?"

"Don't you think worrying helps you prepare?"

"Maybe. Or maybe it just messes you up."

Ronan had a point, but Elizabeth at age nine had realized that if she didn't take care of Mabel, no one else would.

"Mabel almost died when she was a baby because the foster mother we lived with wouldn't take her to the hospital. Too lazy and too drunk, but Mabel was really sick. I tried to steal the neighbor's car and take her there, but the neighbor caught me. Fortunately, he was a nice guy, and drove us there himself. He was a fireman, and he knew people in the emergency room. Good thing." Elizabeth laughed a little. "I was a shrimp and couldn't reach the pedals."

Ronan's eyes held anger. "I hope you didn't stay with that woman."

"No, we were moved. I never did learn the fireman's name, and I never saw him again. But he made me realize there were good people and bad people out there. You have to figure out which is which, but good ones are there. Like you."

Elizabeth put her hand on Ronan's where he rested it on her shoulder, her fingers small against his big, blunt ones.

"What makes you think I'm one of the good ones?" he asked.

"You stopped Marquez, for one. He had a gun—you couldn't know whether he'd have shot you dead. And letting us stay here, eating your food and taking up space. And what you do for the kids—I mean, the cubs." Elizabeth stroked Olaf's fur again. "I'd have been able to tell right away if you mistreated them. But I know they're happy."

Ronan spread his fingers and twined hers between them. "You were like them, weren't you?"

"A rescue case? Pretty much. Only I never got rescued. There were good times, don't get me wrong. It wasn't all terrible. We lived in some good houses, made friends."

"You rescued yourself, Lizzie," Ronan said. He squeezed her fingers, the pressure warm. "But I don't mind coming to your rescue."

Elizabeth squeezed back, feeling the warmth travel all the way through her body. "Why did you stop Liam from questioning me?"

"Because Liam's dangerous," Ronan said. "He and Sean have that Irish charm thing going, but don't underestimate them. They can be hard-ass if they want to be, and their dad's worse. Me mate-claiming you means you'll never be handed over to their dad. It means I've got your back."

With his strong arm behind her shoulders, Elizabeth started to believe it.

"I promise you, Ronan, my secrets won't hurt anyone except me and Mabel. It's because of Mabel that I don't want to tell you."

"WitSec?" Ronan asked.

Elizabeth started. "What?"

"Are you in witness protection? I won't out you, but I don't need a Fed breathing down my neck when one comes looking for you."

"No." She shook her head, squeezing her eyes shut. "Call it Elizabeth protection." She opened her eyes again. "Yes, I moved here six years ago with a new name and a new name for Mabel, but not because I'm running from the law or in witness protection or because I owe people lot of money. I just needed . . . to start again."

He regarded her quietly, keeping whatever emotions he felt hidden. "People can start again without changing their identities. Usually they change identities when they don't want anyone from their past finding them."

Elizabeth said nothing. Ronan was close to the truth, but Elizabeth had learned the hard way that saying nothing was the best thing, no matter what it made people think of her. If she opened up to Ronan, would Liam compel him to tell Elizabeth's secrets? He'd said that this mate-claim protected her from that, but she was sure the smooth-talking Liam would probably find some loophole. Liam seemed to be good at getting his own way.

But Ronan, she'd seen, despite his brawn and good-natured banter, was not stupid. He studied her now with shrewd perception. "You don't have to tell me, Elizabeth. You wait until you're ready. And if it's never, then it's never."

"It won't be never."

Ronan brought their clasped hands up and rubbed her cheek with his broad finger. "The bears in this house have been through a lot. I've learned not to force them to talk about it. You take your time."

Elizabeth turned her head to find herself nose-to-nose with him. "I used to be a very bad judge of character, is all." Elizabeth slid her hand to his neck, playing with the ends of his very short hair. She liked how it felt, prickly but soft, like Olaf's fur. Under that was his Collar, warm metal fused to his neck. "But I've become much better at it," she said softly.

"And I'm one of the good ones?"

For answer, Elizabeth leaned in and kissed him.

It started as a small kiss, a thank-you kiss, but Ronan's big hand came around her neck, and he slanted his mouth over hers. His answering kiss was strong, warm, responsive.

Elizabeth parted her lips, her body tightening as his tongue swept into her mouth. His strength took her breath away, but he gentled it for her, holding back. Holding back a lot. The wildness in him, tempered for her, excited her.

He kissed slowly, firmly, his lips smooth. Elizabeth let her fingers slide down his back, finding muscles so solid they didn't give under her fingers. His hand on her neck never moved, as though he held her up, as though she'd never fall as long as he was with her.

Elizabeth moved closer. She kissed him hungrily, needing to know he'd hold her up forever.

On her lap, Olaf stirred and emitted a little growl.

Ronan eased from the kiss but didn't release her. He held her, their faces almost touching, his eyes so dark. A spark winked deep within them.

*I can take care of myself.* This was Elizabeth's constant mantra. But wouldn't it be wonderful to surrender to strength such as Ronan had, to know she would be safe—for always?

"We should put him to bed," Ronan said.

Olaf. He was warm on her lap, sleeping soundly. Elizabeth didn't want to let him go.

"You have a bed for baby polar bears?"

"He'll shift back."

Ronan pressed a last, soft kiss to Elizabeth's mouth, rose, and lifted Olaf. The cub didn't move and didn't change shape. Ronan signaled to Elizabeth to follow, and he carried the bear out of the living room and up the stairs.

The largest front room was taken by the two male cubs and held the detritus of boys of two ages: magazines, CDs, posters, toy trucks, action figures. No video games and no TV, because Shifters weren't allowed much technology. A small computer stood in one corner, an older model. That was all.

Both beds were fairly big and very sturdy. Elizabeth saw why when Ronan laid Olaf on one. He curled up, the claws of one paw slicing the cover of the pillow. From all the rents on the pillow, he'd done that more than once.

Ronan dragged a cover over him. "If he shifts back in his sleep, he'll get cold," he explained. He lingered to rest his large hand on Olaf's shoulder.

Under his touch, Olaf took a deep breath, and then shifted effortlessly back to the small boy with blue-streaked blond hair. He opened his eyes. "Lizbeth?"

"I'm right here." Elizabeth leaned down and kissed his cheek. "Good night, Olaf."

Olaf caught her hand in a surprisingly strong grip. "Stay."

"She's got to go to bed, Oláf," Ronan said. "She's tired."

Olaf's eyes took on a glint of panic Elizabeth had sometimes seen in Mabel's when Mabel had been little. Mabel's greatest terror had been that she'd go to sleep and wake up alone, Elizabeth gone, never to be found again. Olaf, Ronan had said, had seen his parents killed. That terror had come true for him.

"No," Olaf said. "Stay."

"It's all right." Elizabeth sat down on the large bed, Olaf not letting go of her hand. "I don't mind. He's scared."

"He has to learn he'll be all right," Ronan said.

Olaf's grip tightened even more. He would have wrestler strength when he grew up, greater maybe even than Ronan's.

"Does he have to learn tonight? I don't mind."

Ronan stood over them, hands on hips, a frustrated parent. "All right, all right. But only tonight."

Elizabeth lay down on the bed behind Olaf and pulled the cover over her, kicking her loose shoes to the floor. Olaf snuggled back against her and looked up at Ronan.

"Stay too," he said.

Ronan heaved a sigh. "Becks is spoiling you. Fine, big guy. We'll both stay."

He collapsed onto Scott's empty bed, which creaked under his weight, then shucked his belt and shoes and pulled quilts over his big body.

Olaf fell asleep quickly, but Elizabeth remained awake next to him, still feeling the imprint of Ronan's kiss. Her life was changing dramatically as she watched, and she needed to make decisions.

Ronan, up most of the night before, all day at the store, and then again tonight, fell asleep quickly. He snored. Rebecca hadn't been kidding. Not snorting wet-sounding snores, but deep, steady ones, his breath going all the way to the bottom of his lungs and coming all the way out again.

The sound didn't bother Elizabeth. It was comforting. A huge, strong man slept near her, on hand to defend her. Ronan was a swift, silent killer, and a protector, and beneath all that, he had a heart of vast generosity. Elizabeth in the past had been duped by people who'd pretended to be kind, but Ronan was kind while pretending not to be.

Elizabeth drifted off to sleep so gradually she didn't know she was doing it, but all through the night, she heard the solidity of Ronan's snores, and knew she was guarded.

*** *** ***

Sundays, Elizabeth always closed the store but went to work in the back, getting ready for the week to come. Ronan went in with her, and Ellison and Spike came to fix the bear-shaped hole in her door.

Rebecca had returned while Ronan and Elizabeth breakfasted with the ravenous Olaf, Rebecca looking tired but pleased with herself. She was wearing a "Keep Austin Weird" T-shirt that hadn't been on her when she left.

"Good shopping trip, I take it?" Elizabeth said, licking honey from her fork.

"Oh, yeah." Rebecca yawned, stretched, and went upstairs to shower.

Scott came home before Elizabeth and Ronan left, as did Cherie and Mabel. Cherie and Mabel were chipper; Scott mumbled something and shuffled upstairs to his bedroom.

Olaf wanted to see the store, but Elizabeth, uncertain that Marquez or his friends wouldn't return, said no. Olaf was disappointed, but he agreed, with surprising cheerfulness, to wait until Ronan thought it safe.

"He trusts you," Elizabeth said as she and Ronan headed out for Ronan's motorcycle.

"Olaf? Mostly. He just gets scared at night. You sleep okay?"

"Yes." She had. In spite of the late night and early start, Elizabeth felt refreshed. In the room with Olaf and Ronan, she'd let herself completely relax for the first time in . . . well, forever.

Spike and Ellison were waiting outside the store when they arrived. Ellison lounged on the hood of his pickup, a long, tall Texan if Elizabeth ever saw one, though Ronan had told her he'd come here from Colorado.

Spike looked pure urban biker. He leaned against the wall outside the store, skin well inked, sunglasses against the glare, and motorcycle boots and grease-stained jeans to Ellison's cowboy boots. This morning, though, one side of his face was purple and black, and when he took off his sunglasses, his left eye definitely sported a shiner.

"What happened to you?" Elizabeth asked.

"Fight club." Spike shrugged tight shoulders. "Don't tell Liam."

Elizabeth wanted to ask, but other store owners were looking out their doors at the Shifters. Elizabeth got the store unlocked and them inside as quickly as she could.

"Fight club?" she asked Ronan as Ellison and Spike carried toolboxes to the torn-up wall. The two

Shifters started pondering how to fix it in the universal male way of standing back and staring at it.

Ronan didn't look very surprised at her question. "Liam gets pissed off, because he says it's glorified cock fighting, and he's right. But he doesn't stop Shifters going—the fights allow us to let off steam. Fight clubs are privately arranged bouts between Shifters, no holds barred. Not exactly legal, but humans bet on us, and we give them a good show, so there's a lot of looking the other way."

"Like gladiators." Elizabeth's gaze went to the Collar snug against Ronan's big neck, the Celtic knot at his throat. "Don't your Collars stop you?"

"Oh, they go off. Believe me. It evens the field, Shifter against Shifter. Some are better than others at fighting through the pain. Spike's one of the favorites. Trust me, the other guy will look worse."

Elizabeth stared at him. "You have to be crazy. I've seen underground boxing and mixed martial arts meets, and they're brutal. Shifter ones have to be even more brutal."

"They can be. But Shifters are tough, Elizabeth. And sometimes we have to fight, or we go a little nuts. Humans think they suppress our fighting instincts with the Collars, but the instincts don't go away. Except that now, we have no natural outlet. So Liam pretends he doesn't see a dozen Shifters disappear at night and come back bruised and Collar-wasted. Even Scott's been going lately."

"And you *let* him? Ronan . . ."

"He's a Shifter going through his Transition. Scott wants to fight all the time these days—at the fight clubs, at least, the other Shifters let him work it off, and they take care of him."

Elizabeth rubbed her forehead. "The more I learn about you, the more I realize I don't know. I was right in the first place. You're crazy."

Ronan grinned, the warm one that lit his eyes. "Yeah, but crazy in a good way."

"You take a big risk telling me this. You've told me a lot of things I could report to the human cops, you know. I wouldn't, but why do you trust that I won't?"

Ronan drew a finger along one of the red streaks in Elizabeth's hair. "Because I know," he said in his quiet voice. "You're one of the good ones."

Elizabeth's body heated instantly at his touch. She thought of lying in the dark with him nearby all night, loving having him there. This was getting dangerous.

A whistle pierced the air, and Elizabeth, nerves frayed, jumped. "What was that?"

"Signal," Ronan said, turning away. "Trackers have spotted something."

Her fears returned. "What?"

Ronan looked out the tiny back window, scanning the alley. "Come on. Stay close to me."

Ellison and Spike had stopped hammering and drilling and came into the office. Spike retained his hammer as he went to the back door and opened it.

Two Latino men, one about six foot, the other a head shorter, stood in front of a silver gray Lexus parked a yard from Elizabeth's door. Both men wore dark suits on this late August day. They weren't obviously armed, but the suit coats could hide anything. Both stood casually, alert but not hostile.

Spike went out first, then Ronan, with Elizabeth between Ronan and Ellison. As they emerged, three more Shifters entered the other end of the alley— Sean with his sword, a Shifter as tall as he who looked much like him, and an even taller Shifter male with his black hair buzzed short. The two human men saw the Shifters but didn't change expression.

The taller of the men nodded at Elizabeth. "Elizabeth Chapman. I'm Pablo Marquez."

Elizabeth had suspected as much. She said nothing.

"The incident with my brother has caused some problems," Marquez said in a smooth voice. "He didn't come here that night with my blessing. It was a stupid thing to do."

Elizabeth still remained silent. She knew that a man like Marquez could twist anything she said into either capitulation or a threat, so it was best to stand quietly and let him talk.

"I'm taking care of Julio," Marquez went on. "He knows how pissed off I am. But it leaves us with a little problem. He's facing charges of armed robbery, and there are two witnesses. You and your Shifter."

Ronan moved in front of Marquez and folded his arms. In spite of Marquez's relative tallness, Ronan was twice his size.

Sean and the other two Shifters drifted toward them, but not in a clump. They spaced themselves out so the one with the black hair stayed at the opening of the alley, Sean stopped about halfway down, and the third man came to a stop right behind Marquez's car.

"Your brother almost killed Elizabeth," Ronan said. "That pisses me off too."

Marquez looked up at Ronan's nearly seven-foot height without fear. "You're the Shifter who took him down?"

"I wasn't out to kill him. I only meant to stop him."

"I figured that," Marquez said. "You're a Shifter. If you'd wanted to kill him, Julio would be dead. But, see, he's my brother. I don't want him in prison. Not only would that be dangerous for him, it would be bad for business."

Elizabeth understood his concern—there might be plenty in prison with a grudge against Marquez who would use his younger brother as an opportunistic target. But she only had so much sympathy.

"So, what are you saying?" she asked. "We can come to some sort of arrangement?"

"I want to make a deal, yes," Marquez said. "Julio's going to trial—he's been released in my custody but he has a court date. Which he will keep. What I'm asking is for you not to show up. You and your sister close up shop and leave town, start over some other place. I'll put the word out ahead that you're not to be bothered. But you go, never come back to Austin, never talk to anyone about Julio and Pablo Marquez."

"Leave?" Elizabeth started for him, but Ronan dodged in her way. His Collar emitted one spark. "I can't leave," Elizabeth said. "I worked my ass off for this store. I'm not moving my whole life because your little brother is out of control."

"You haven't heard the other half of my deal," Marquez said, his hard voice breaking through hers. "You go and start again somewhere safe, or you have no life at all. Neither does your sister. I won't bother trying to scare you or harass you, or any juvenile shit like that. You're either alive in another city, or dead here. Nothing in between. I'll give you three days to pack and shut down. Then you're gone."

Ronan leaned in to Marquez. "Here's our counteroffer. *You* leave town, you let your brother go to prison for what he did, or *your* life will be a living hell. *We'll* put word out ahead wherever you go that you shouldn't be bothered, but you'll be watched. You're now on every Shifter's shit list, which is someplace you don't want to be."

Marquez didn't move. "You're Shifters. You're powerless. Shifters are executed for harming humans. You lay a finger on me, the whole bunch of you goes down. I don't even have to ask for a hit. The cops will do it for me."

"That's our offer," Ronan said. "If you want to get out of this alley alive, you'll give us your answer."

Marquez opened his coat to show that he had an automatic in his shoulder holster. "These sweeties will take you out quickly, leaving nothing but dead Shifters behind. You can't move fast enough to dodge bullets, and your Collars mean you can't attack me. So. I'll leave you to make your decision, Ms. Chapman. I understand about family. For your sister's sake, you'll go."

Elizabeth did not like the look of that weapon, but Ronan scarcely seemed to notice it. "Your answer," he said.

Marquez's hand drifted toward his gun, but—so swiftly Elizabeth didn't see him move— the Shifter who resembled Sean was in front of Marquez, hand on Marquez's wrist.

Marquez's eyes widened as the Shifter put pressure on the wrist, and Elizabeth heard something crackle. Marquez's man reached inside his coat, but Marquez shook his head, though his eyes were nearly bulging. The Shifter's Collar didn't so much as glint, and he said not a word.

Sean spoke without moving his position. "We'll give you a day or two to think about it, lad. Then it's best you go. We'll make sure nothing happens to your brother inside. We know about family too."

The Shifter kept his hold of Marquez's wrist. Marquez looked up into his cold, cold eyes, and finally showed fear.

"Let him go, Dad," Sean said.

The Shifter opened his hand and took a step back. He was very calm, every movement precise and practiced.

Marquez backed a step and cradled his wrist but he gave Elizabeth a cool stare. "You lost yourself a day," he said. "Pack and go."

The second man, who looked white about the mouth, opened the passenger side of the car and let in Marquez. Marquez didn't look at the Shifters as the man went around to the driver's seat, got in and started the Lexus, then slowly pulled forward. Ronan, Spike, Ellison, and the other Shifter moved so the car could pass, but they surrounded it to watch it go, hunters releasing their prey. Their choice. For now.

As soon as the car turned the corner onto the street, Sean joined them and said, "Nice one, Dad."

Elizabeth rounded on them. "Nice one? Are you all insane? All he has to do is report that you threatened him. Criminal or not, you're the ones who'll pay—with your lives. Do me a favor, and *don't help me!*"

Elizabeth's rage and fear had risen to a breaking point, and all she could do was turn her back on the Shifters, storm inside, and slam the door.

# Chapter Ten

Ronan scented Elizabeth's terror as she went, and vowed that Marquez would pay for every bad dream, every shiver of fear, and every tear he'd caused her.

Sean joined his father, whose eyes remained the light blue of his wildcat's. "You scared him good, Dad," Sean said. "But maybe put him on his guard? We don't need a Shifter-human gang war."

"We won't have one." Dylan Morrissey scanned the alley, aware that others could be watching, and started for the back door to Elizabeth's store.

Ronan got ahead of him to walk inside first, but Elizabeth wasn't in her office. Ronan heard the water running in the bathroom, and he left the others to approach her.

He'd lived with females long enough to know that if he knocked first, she'd tell him to go away and leave her alone, and he had no intention of doing that. Elizabeth hadn't locked the door, however, and Ronan opened it to find a small bathroom decorated with rose trellis wallpaper and framed Victorian ads for soap and chocolates. The soft colors made the tiny room easy on the eyes and very feminine.

Elizabeth looked up at him through the reflection of the wooden framed mirror over the sink, her eyes red-rimmed, her face dripping.

"You okay?" Ronan asked.

A long time ago, he'd never had to worry about comforting crying females — crying anybody. But now he had to deal with Cherie with her PTSD, Rebecca's PMS, and the terror dreams of the boys. He'd learned how to pet and hold until the shakes went away, how to gentle his voice to the merest rumble.

"No, I'm not okay," Elizabeth said. "You can't threaten Marquez like that. He's right — he'll have the cops down on you, or he'll tell his boys with machine guns to wipe out all the Shifters. No one cares about Shifters."

"That's true," Ronan said, leaning against the door frame. "No one, except Shifters. What do you plan to do, then? Leave town like he suggested?"

"No!" Elizabeth grabbed a fluffy towel and buried her face in it. When she emerged, her tears were gone. "No, I'm not letting him drive me out. I'll call the cop who arrested Julio Marquez and tell her his brother is threatening me. Pablo Marquez will have a record — they can put a restraining order on him."

"A restraining order will do nothing," Dylan said from behind Ronan. "You need to let us take care of this."

Elizabeth threw down the towel and pushed past Ronan to face Dylan. "Let you take care of it? What does that mean?" She looked up at the tall Shifter, meeting that white-blue stare without flinching.

Sean cleared his throat. "Ms. Chapman, let me introduce my dad, Dylan Morrissey."

Elizabeth studied Dylan more closely, taking in the gray at his temples, his stern look that came with his years and experience. "Ah. I've heard about you."

Dylan blinked, his eyes snapping back to human blue. Elizabeth's *I've heard about you* spoke volumes. His mate, Glory, came into this store a lot, and Glory could be earthily frank. Dylan must be wondering what the hell kinds of things Glory had said.

"What I've heard is that you're used to having your every order obeyed," Elizabeth said, hands on hips. "But I'm not Shifter, and I don't care. I'm keeping this store open. I'm grateful for your help, but I do not want you confronting Marquez. He's dangerous, more dangerous than you are. I'll find a solution. I haven't survived this long by caving in to people like him."

Sean and the other Shifters tensed, watching as Elizabeth, a puny human, stared down one of the top alphas in Shiftertown. Liam was leader now, yes, but Dylan was still plenty dominant.

Ronan went warm with pride. His potential mate had moxie.

She didn't understand, though, that she and Dylan were talking about two different things. Elizabeth was thinking about her immediate future, keeping hold of the things for which she'd worked so hard. Dylan was considering the threat Marquez posed to Shifters in general, outside Marquez's problem with Elizabeth. The situation had moved beyond the attempted robbery and into wider realms.

Dylan moved his gaze from Elizabeth to Ronan. "She's your responsibility," he said.

"I know that," Ronan answered.

Dylan held Ronan with his gaze for a long moment, then he signaled to Sean and the other tracker—Nate—and the three of them departed. No good-byes, no saying where they were going. They simply went.

Elizabeth watched them go, hands still planted on her slim hips, then she swung to Spike and Ellison. "All right, then," she growled. "That wall isn't fixing itself. Let's get back to work."

*** *** ***

Pablo Marquez employed the best lookouts in the city, but for some reason they totally missed the Shifters that materialized in his office that evening. One minute Pablo was going over his spreadsheets for the body shop; the next, he had three Shifters around his desk.

Pablo didn't panic. He hadn't gotten this far in life by panicking. He smoothly brought his hand out from under the desk, wrist now wrapped in an ace bandage, an automatic weapon nestled against his palm. He held the gun loosely, not pointing it or threatening with it. Shifters were dangerous, yes, but they weren't immune to bullets.

The one with the terrifying eyes was there, but as he'd done in the alley, he remained silent. The guy with the sword, obviously the Shifter's son, stepped in front of the desk, putting himself directly in front of Pablo's gun. Ballsy of him. The third Shifter, the one with the military-cut black hair, watched the door with seeming negligence. He was chewing gum, a trick for indicating contempt and lack of fear.

Pablo made the opening sally. "I said all I had to say. If you try to force me to leave with you, you'll walk into twenty of my boys with pistols, ready to take you down. You're not like werewolves who die only by silver bullets. Lots of lead will do the trick." He lounged back in his chair, relaxed. No need to chew gum to prove it. "You're in my territory now."

"Not quite." The guy with the sword—Sean Morrissey—Pablo had looked him up—rested big hands on the desk. "You are in *our* territory. Shifter territory."

"Shifters live in Shiftertowns," Pablo said. "That's all the territory you get."

His father—Dylan, the guy's name was—finally spoke. His voice was a little different from his son's, as cold and hard, yes, but with vast stillness behind it. This was a man who'd seen much, done much, suffered more than Pablo's group of hardened thugs could imagine. What Pablo wouldn't give to have this man as a resource.

"The entire city is Shifter territory," Dylan was saying. "Our lands run from San Marcos to north and west of the lake. Hill Country Shifters take over from there."

Pablo barked a laugh. "In your Shifter dreams. Trust me, I'm not a guy who likes to follow other people's rules. I do what I want and deal with what I have to. I also think the humans who have basically neutered you are amazingly stupid. They could have used you to help them fight wars or to put down people like me, but you know governments. Full of people who can't get real jobs. But they slapped those Collars on you and pretty much broke whatever power you had, although from what I can tell it wasn't very much to begin with. You have no territory, my friends. You have nothing."

None of the Shifters moved during his speech. No scorn, no anger, no conceding that he might be right. Nothing but three pairs of Shifter eyes fixed on him.

To keep them from overwhelming him, Pablo sorted them out. Sean and Dylan were father and son. The big sword Sean wore wasn't for killing, Pablo had learned, but for some sort of death ritual, the blade stuck into the Shifter after he was dead.

The guy with the military haircut Pablo had seen at the very illegal Shifter fight clubs where Shifters fought each other for fun and other people bet on them. The guy's name was Nate, and his friend Spike, the one with all the tattoos, was a very popular fighter.

"What do you want, boys?" Pablo asked. "To bargain? I'm afraid I hold all the bargaining chips."

The one called Sean leaned his fists on the desk. The wood, a nice mahogany, creaked.

"I'm afraid Dad wants you out, lad. The fact that he came down here to ask you nicely is unusual. My advice to you? Move your enterprise to another city. Ronan told you, we'll inform the Shifters around wherever you choose to go to leave you alone—if you behave yourself, that is."

"We've done this dance," Pablo said. "Your threat doesn't have teeth . . . so to speak."

"That's because we don't like to show our hand too soon. You, my good friend—well, you don't know what you're up against. My dad there, he's not such a reasonable man. I am. That's why they always send me to negotiate."

"But I'm not negotiating anything," Pablo said.

Sean gave him a smile. Why did Pablo think of a cat drawing back its lips to show its teeth? "Well, that's fine, because we're not negotiating, either," Sean said. "The truth is, lad, if you don't go now, there'll be nothing left for you."

"Nothing left of what?" Always difficult to guard against vague threats. Vague threats made everyone paranoid and sleepless. Pablo knew that because he often employed the technique himself.

Sean shrugged. "Of anything. You, this nice building, your boys outside, your fine car. All gone." He leaned closer. "In the blink of an eye."

Pablo moved his gun slightly, reminding Sean that it was there. "And if I mow you down before you can leave?"

"Won't matter. My brother, now, he's the vindictive one. My dad's learned to control himself a bit, but we're not so sure about Liam. And we all have family that wouldn't be too happy with you if anything happened to us."

Pablo made sure his finger was obviously off the trigger. "I've been in this game a long time, Shifter. There's always someone out there with a vendetta. I don't let it worry me."

"Son," Sean said, in an almost kind voice. "You wouldn't have time to let it worry you."

Pablo was not blind to the fact that these guys were serious. Somehow, they'd gotten past his guards. He had no doubt that if he killed them, three more Shifters would visit him in the night. Collars or no Collars, laws or no laws, they knew their stuff.

He took his hand all the way off the gun and pushed the pistol aside, leaving it close enough to grab if he needed to, but showing that he'd be happy to settle this without violence. Which he was. Julio had been stupid, and even Pablo hadn't realized that the bitch had the entire Austin Shiftertown backing her up. Julio so needed to learn to do his research first.

Pablo had been researching Elizabeth Chapman ever since Julio had gotten himself arrested for trying to rob her. He'd run into difficulty trying to discover specifics about her past, but he'd find out. He was very close.

"I don't have time for a war," Pablo said in a reasonable tone. "And I'm thinking neither do you. My brother is an idiot, but I have some good lawyers, and maybe I can get him out of this. But it will be bad for my business if your friends insist on testifying."

"Your business really isn't our concern," Sean said. "Don't you sell drugs and hurt people? Not a business we want in our town."

Pablo's business was a little more sophisticated than that, but he wasn't going to argue the point.

"How about this?" he asked. "Your friend gets a little forgetful in the witness box, my lawyers help my brother, and we call it quits? Your friend stays in her business in SoCo, I stay in mine here, and we never see each other again."

The Shifters said nothing. They didn't look at one another, but Pablo got the feeling they were discussing it amongst themselves, with that nonverbal communication animals were supposed to have.

The one called Dylan was the first to speak. "We want you out of our town, Pablo Marquez. And you'll go."

He looked straight into Pablo's eyes. Pablo, having grown up in the back streets of almost every city in the south, had learned to meet his opponent's challenging stare and then look away casually, almost derisively, as though he wasn't concerned about winning the staring contest.

But he couldn't look away from Dylan. Pablo wanted to, but Dylan's blue-white stare would not let him go. He saw, behind Dylan, Sean relaxed, unworried. They had no doubt that Pablo would obey Dylan — if not now, then eventually.

"Why don't you go on out of here?" Pablo said, pretending nonchalance. "I'll make sure my boys don't get trigger happy so you make it to your car. But I can't guarantee it, so watch yourselves."

The Shifters didn't like being dismissed. Well, too bad. Pablo wasn't going to wet himself for them. He had his own plans. The next time they met, he wouldn't be caught so unprepared.

They faded away. Pablo wasn't sure how they did it, but one minute the three Shifters were in the shadows of his office; the next, they were gone.

He snapped an order to the man who was supposed to guard the door and got no response. Gun in hand, Pablo made his way to the front door and peered outside. The darkening street showed no one, not his guards, not retreating Shifters, not the mechanics who ostensibly worked in his body shop. All was silence, but for the few bits of trash that drifted across the pavement on a hot Texas wind.

# Chapter Eleven

The bar Liam managed opened for business that night, but none of the Shifters went to work. Ronan explained that the human government had ruled that Shifters did not have to work on Sundays, a concession to the Shifters' request that they be able to continue their religious observances after taking the Collars. Ronan related this with a laugh, because, he said, Shifters didn't have a designated religious day or a set time for prayer. All days were religious to them; any time and place fine for meditation and prayer.

An interesting take on the matter, Elizabeth thought.

Apparently Shifters used the day off to build bonfires in the common land between the backs of their houses, cook out, and let the kids run around in both human and animal form.

Sean Morrissey, minus sword and in a plain T-shirt, was grilling alongside his brother Liam, the two of them arguing about how best to cook the steaks. Ellison and the trackers lounged nearby, beers in hand, though Spike with his black eye wasn't getting too close to Liam.

Cherie and Mabel were laughing together in the age-old manner of twenty-something girls aware that men eyed them, but not deigning to notice. Olaf romped around in his bear cub form with wolf cubs and wildcat cubs.

The tall, blonde Glory sat on her porch, long legs crossed, in a tight, leopard-print pantsuit, not far from Dylan, who quietly drank beer from a dark bottle. With them were Kim and little Katriona and the pregnant Andrea.

Elizabeth eyed them a little shyly. They were all so comfortable with each other, including Kim, who was human, an outsider. Mabel carried on as though she'd lived here all her life, but then, that was Mabel. Elizabeth had always been the cautious one.

Ronan moved close to her. "I know."

Elizabeth looked up in surprise. "Know what?"

He motioned to the scene around them. "It's overwhelming. You don't know who to get close to, who to talk to. You want to be accepted, but it's a little scary with all those eyes looking at you. You don't want to say the wrong thing to the wrong person."

"Exactly. Are you reading my mind or something?"

"Your body language." Ronan's warm hand rested on the small of her back. "And it's how I felt when I first moved in."

"You?" Elizabeth studied the towering man, with his round, tight shoulders in his T-shirt. "You were shy?"

"I'd lived by myself in the Alaskan woods all my life. Most of my life, anyway. Then I was shoved into a Shiftertown with all these wolves and wildcats who stared at me all the time. I'm a big guy, and that makes it worse."

"You stand out." Elizabeth snaked her arm around his waist. "Hard to miss."

"You got that right."

"And then you adopted a bunch of cubs." She shook her head in mock dismay as they strolled away from Glory's house. "What were you thinking?"

"I ask myself that sometimes."

Elizabeth hooked her fingers through his belt loop, liking how the loop seemed to be made for her fingers. "So where do you go when you want to be alone? Really alone?"

"Around here? It's tough. I've got the Den, but that's always being invaded. But there are some caves out west of town, down on the riverbank. Not many people know about them. I go out there, sometimes. Not the same as the deep woods, but it can be peaceful."

"Sounds nice," Elizabeth said wistfully. "I never have time to go to places like that."

"I'll take you. You'll make time."

"Then you won't be by yourself. I thought that was the point."

They'd cleared the crowd and were now relatively isolated under tall Texas oak trees. Ronan stopped. "I won't mind being alone there with you."

Elizabeth let go of his belt loop and turned to face him. It felt right to put her hands on his waist, to feel the warmth of his big body through her fingertips.

Ronan's eyes went dark. "I'm going to kiss you, Elizabeth," he said, a growl in his voice. "I've been dying to kiss you all day."

"Yeah? What stopped you?"

"Human gang leaders and too many nosy Shifters."

"There aren't any around right now." Trees screened them from the Shifter gathering and the bonfires' glows.

For answer, Ronan leaned to her, his breath touching her mouth, his lips following. He kissed her softly, as though afraid he'd break her, all the while holding her with hands so strong.

Elizabeth pushed up on tiptoes to reach him. "You're so tall," she whispered. "Can't you shrink a little?"

Ronan's smile warmed his eyes as he slid his arm behind her buttocks and lifted her off her feet.

He held her securely in powerful arms, his chest like a wall. Elizabeth wrapped her legs around his waist, arms around his back. Much, much better.

They were face to face. Ronan brushed his lips to the corner of her mouth, then licked there. "I'm not used to kissing humans," he said. "Hell, I don't kiss many Shifters. I don't want to hurt you," he finished, brow furrowing.

She nuzzled his cheek, liking the roughness of his whiskers. She kissed his nose where it had been broken. "I'm pretty resilient."

He lost his smile. "No, you're not. You're so vulnerable. Elizabeth, I'm sorry."

"For what?"

"For not killing that idiot with the gun and then taking you back to Alaska with me. It's beautiful there. I had a cabin in the woods, right next to this stream that roars all the time—even in the winter you can hear it gurgling under the ice. It's an amazing place. You'd love it."

"But they forced you out, didn't they?" Elizabeth asked softly. "That's why you're here."

"I got rounded up when Shifters were outed twenty years ago. A couple of people knew there was a Shifter living back in the woods, and one told the police." He sighed. "I'd counted them as friends, but one sniff of a reward for Shifters . . ."

"I'm so sorry." Elizabeth's fury rose for whoever had betrayed him. She remembered the witch hunts for Shifters twenty years ago, though she'd been only a kid at the time, with too many problems of her own to pay much attention. When humans had realized that shapeshifters were real and living among them, they'd reacted with paranoia. Instead of trying to understand the Shifters, they'd rounded them up, killed some, done experiments on others, confined them, slapped Collars on them to control their violence, and heavily restricted them. Only because of the actions of some equal rights groups were Shifters allowed to live at all.

How anyone could have handed over this wonderful, warmhearted man to be locked away, far from his home, Elizabeth didn't understand. Ronan craved solitude but gladly gave it up to help those in need, with no other incentive than he felt bad for them. She'd learned, the hard way, the difference between people who practiced charity to look good and the people who were truly caring.

"I told you, Ronan," she said. "You're one of the good ones."

"Aw. Bet you say that to all the bears."

"Just the big wrestler ones I want to kiss."

"Shut up and kiss me, then."

Ronan held her in arms that never moved as their mouths met, touched, explored. Elizabeth's body heated, and her limbs relaxed with longing.

She wanted to be alone with him, and she wanted to make love to him.

The thought stunned her. Elizabeth broke the kiss, her face an inch from his, their breaths tangling. But then, maybe it wasn't so astonishing. She wanted to be alone with him, so see his body bare for her, to feel his weight on her as he made love to her. Ronan made a noise like a growl, his eyes holding a hunger that matched her own.

They heard the kids playing, Olaf's small roar as he ran with the other cubs, Rebecca admonishing, "Stay close to the porch, Olaf."

Ronan touched his forehead to hers. "No one will be at the house," he said.

Elizabeth nodded, her need for him overwhelming. Ronan unlocked her legs from around him and slid her to her feet. She felt the hardness of him on the way down, and her eyes widened. Ronan was a big guy, and she'd heard rumors about Shifters. Knowing she'd soon see whether they were true made her shiver in excitement.

They walked away from the crowd, hand in hand, Elizabeth's heart beating in time with their swift pace. She liked this, the two of them wanting the same thing, united in their unspoken longing. They needed privacy for it, but they also knew that they could return to friends and family anytime they liked.

Ronan's house was dark, but he didn't take Elizabeth inside. Instead, he led her down the side path to the Den.

When he turned on the light, Elizabeth saw that this was a decidedly masculine hangout. The big room contained a television, kitchenette with a big refrigerator — probably well-stocked with beer — shelves stacked with games, a couple of card tables, and a gigantic bed covered with an equally gigantic quilt.

Ronan swept up Elizabeth and carried her, romance-style, to the bed. He followed her down to the mattress and lay on his side next to her, eyes dark. He ran his hand down her arm, ending by cradling her hip.

"I thought it was the mate-claim making me crazy," he said. "Starting the mating frenzy. But it's just you." He released her hip and trailed his fingers up her torso, between her breasts. "You're amazing. And I want to see that tattoo."

He hooked his fingers on the neckline of her shirt, pulling it down a little to bare the butterfly that ran along her collarbone. Elizabeth stilled under Ronan's touch, loving the warm need that filled her, a kind she'd never felt before. She wanted to wrap herself around him and pull him down to her, kiss him until her cravings were fulfilled. But she remained motionless, marveling in the light brush of his fingertips on her skin.

Ronan traced the butterfly once with his fingers, then leaned down and traced it with his tongue. Elizabeth closed her eyes, body loosening, surrendering.

A crazed roar had her nearly flying up out of the bed, her tension returning in a rush. Ronan swung his legs around and came to his feet faster than Elizabeth would have guessed such a big man could move.

The roar came again. Loud, deep, animal. Ronan tore open the door and ran into the yard, peeling off his T-shirt as he went. His jeans followed, boots flying. Elizabeth experienced one glorious instant seeing him tall and naked in the moonlight, before his limbs distorted, and the space between house and Den filled with Kodiak bear.

Ronan ran for the second bear who stood on his hind legs in the yard. The bear was snarling, all teeth bared, and as Ronan went at him, the other bear came down and charged.

The black bear was much smaller than the Kodiak, but the black bear didn't care. Its Collar emitted dozens of sparks, which made it roar in pain, but the bear kept running for Ronan, its eyes red, foam dripping from its mouth.

Elizabeth watched, holding her breath, as Ronan ran straight into the black bear, tumbling to the ground with it. Dust exploded as both bears rolled over each other, the black bear snarling with insane intensity.

Ronan's bear fought in deadly silence. The other bear clawed at him mindlessly, roars ringing into the night. Its Collar kept sparking, white hot in the darkness, but Ronan's Collar remained, like him, quiet.

The fight drew attention. A big gray wolf bounded around the house and headed for Elizabeth. The wolf was huge, at least twice the size of an ordinary wolf, and its eyes were white, fur ice-gray in the moonlight. Elizabeth drew back, ready to run for the Den, and then the wolf's limbs rippled and changed. In a few brief moments, she stood face to face with Ellison Rowe, who now wore not a stitch.

"You okay?" Ellison asked, breathing hard.

"Sure." Elizabeth turned to the bears again. Blood showed on Ronan's coat as he struggled to get the other bear under control.

"That's Scott," Ellison said. "The Transition's rough."

The black bear managed to squirm away from the big Kodiak and loped for Elizabeth.

"Shit," Ellison said. His shifting process went in reverse, and the wolf returned, positioning himself in front of Elizabeth and snarling a warning.

Ronan was almost upon the black bear. As Ronan leapt for him, the black bear sidestepped, rolled, shifted in the middle of the roll, and came to his feet as Scott. Naked, muscles rippling, he was long and lean, body honed, but the look in his eyes as he ran at Elizabeth was raw and furious.

Ellison snarled a guttural snarl, all his wolf teeth bared, ears flat on his head. Ronan, behind Scott, shifted to his human self.

Scott kept coming. Ronan closed the distance between himself and the younger man, put his wrestler's arms all the way around Scott, and lifted him off his feet.

Scott fought him. He ripped at Ronan's hold, his Collar sparking like crazy. He butted his head back against Ronan, and blood dripped from Ronan's mouth. Scott's Collar crackled as loud as Ellison's growls, and then Scott screamed.

It was a horrible sound. The scream went on and on, spilling out Scott's anguish and pain, frustration and rage. Ronan held him fast, and Scott kept fighting. Ellison stayed in front of Elizabeth, his growls lessening but his teeth still bared.

Scott's struggles slowed, though his Collar remained a white band around his neck in the dark. As he weakened, Ronan pulled him into his big arms.

"Let it go," Ronan said. "Calm and quiet. Deep breaths, like I taught you."

Scott was sobbing now. The Collar's glow faded, gradually, as Scott continued to cry. Ronan held him close, pressing a kiss to Scott's unruly black hair.

"Is he all right?" Elizabeth started forward, but Ellison, still the wolf, got in her way.

"Stay over there, Lizzie-girl," Ronan said. "He'll be okay."

Scott didn't look okay. He hung in Ronan's arms, weak, his Collar still emitting sparks.

Ellison rose again to become Ellison. He put his hands on his trim hips. "Poor kid. When I went through the Transition, my grandmother would throw a bucket of ice water over me to calm me down. And I didn't have to worry about the Collar back then—this was before Collars were invented."

Across the yard, Ronan spoke to Scott in a low voice, and Scott nodded, head buried in Ronan's shoulder.

"Why did he try to attack Ronan?" Elizabeth asked.

Ellison's eyes glinted. In the moonlight, stark naked, his eyes still as gray as his wolf's, he looked far more animal than human. "He wasn't trying for Ronan, sweet thing. He was going for you, and Ronan was stopping him. I bet he smelled some pheromones running hot in the Den, and they ignited his hair-trigger mating frenzy." Ellison grinned, and Elizabeth swore his teeth were still pointed. "So what were you and Ronan getting up to in there? Hunh, Lizzie-girl?"

# Chapter Twelve

Ronan got Scott to bed, cleaned himself up, and returned downstairs to see that Ellison was making Elizabeth coffee. Ellison at least had pulled on a pair of jeans. Ronan had as well, and here he'd been hoping he'd get *out* of his clothes for Elizabeth.

Ellison, once Ronan gave him a nod that everything was fine, enclosed Elizabeth in a swift good-bye hug then left through the back door. Ronan sat down at the big table and shoved the mug of coffee Ellison had prepared across to Elizabeth.

"He'll be fine," Ronan said. "Sleeping it off. The Collars hurt like a mo-fo, so Scott's going to be down for a while. Sorry about that. I didn't think he would react to us."

"Ellison said he scented pheromones?" Elizabeth sipped her coffee, looking shaken but determined not to let the incident daunt her.

"He did. During Transition, Shifters walk around in a state of heightened sensitivity to . . . everything. Pheromones, fighting instincts, hunger pangs, you name it. Scott probably sensed us getting hot, and his bear brain suddenly decided I was his rival for the warm female in the Den. When he wakes up, he's going to be embarrassed, so go easy on him."

Elizabeth's hands tightened around her mug. "But if he's that easily triggered, is Mabel safe from him? What about Cherie? Even Rebecca? I can't let Mabel stay here with him like that."

"No, no. Mabel will be fine. And Cherie. Scott knows they're cubs. Mabel might not be a kid anymore in human terms, but to Scott she is. Shifters are even more freaked out about touching cubs than humans are. That's ingrained in us, even during the Transition. As for Rebecca . . ." Ronan had to shake his head. "She's a big Kodiak, like me, and she doesn't take shit from anyone. She's already knocked Scott clear across the house a couple of times. He mostly leaves her alone. But you." Ronan's amusement faded. "I think you'd better stay with Sean and Andrea. I didn't realize a human would trigger the frenzy. But then, I don't know much about humans."

"I trigger a frenzy? No one's ever said that about me before."

Ronan reached for Elizabeth's hand and twined his fingers through hers. "That's why I'm going crazy wanting to touch you." He lifted her fingers to his lips.

"Careful," Elizabeth said softly. "We don't want to upset Scott."

"He's out. Completely out. But I take your point." Ronan kissed each of her fingertips in turn. "I can't seem to stop touching you, Lizzie-girl."

"What are we going to do, then?"

Ronan loved her eyes, so different from a Shifter's, the blue of them pure and dark. "You can accept my mate-claim. Then Scott will know, without doubt, that you belong to me. He won't try to touch you then."

She frowned, brown brows coming together. "How would that work?"

"Honestly?" Ronan shrugged. "I don't know. It's scent, instinct, maybe the pheromones again. We just *know*."

Her fingers lay motionless against his. "What would it mean, exactly? Me accepting your mate-claim?"

He spoke carefully. "It means that you agree to be joined with me in two ceremonies—one under the sun, one under the full moon, in the sight of the Father God and Mother Goddess. But that's only part of it." Ronan leaned across the table to her, inhaling her goodness. "You accepting the mate-claim means that you are mine, and I am yours. We belong to each other. For always." He squeezed her hand. "I'd like that."

Ronan saw longing flare in Elizabeth's eyes, and loneliness, a need to fill the empty spaces in her heart. He also saw fear.

"I've gone down this road before," she said. "I decided then that I'd never let a man have power over me again. It's dangerous. I won't do it."

Ronan felt her terror through their twined hands. He ran his thumb over her fingers, soothing. "This is why you changed your name and started over again, isn't it?"

"Yes." Elizabeth's throat moved. "I got involved with the wrong person, a dangerous one. I didn't realize how dangerous until too late. I only saw a very rich man with a big house who could take care of me, and Mabel too, and he seemed to adore me. That's before I figured out he was a dealer, and into all kinds of very bad things. Mabel was only fifteen, and he was already starting to want her to do favors for his high-flying clients, to sweeten them up. You know what I mean. When I objected, he showed his true colors. He turned into an abusive dickhead, threatening me with all kinds of things, including death, and I realized he'd carry out his threats in truth. The only way I could get away from him was to take Mabel and disappear one afternoon when he was out. I had a friend, from my days in foster care, who knew how to create identities. I gave him a wad of cash, he came up with Elizabeth and Mabel Chapman, and here we are."

Ronan listened, not letting his rage spill over into her fragile hand he still held. "What is his name?" he asked in a quiet voice.

"No, Ronan." Elizabeth's gaze flicked to his, her quiet desperation increasing his anger at whoever this abusive dickhead was. "He's an evil man, and he's surrounded by trigger-happy guards with the latest in firepower. You'd die before you ever saw him."

"I'll never do to you what he did, Lizzie-girl."

"I know." Elizabeth pressed her palm to her chest. "I know that in *here*. My head is still all fucked up."

"Let me explain something," Ronan said in a quiet voice. "To me, you accepting my mate-claim means that I protect you, no matter what. If that includes protecting you from myself, then so be it. I take care of you, I cherish you, I don't let men like Marquez or whoever this asshole is hurt you. You never have to fear them again. Or me, or any Shifter. I'd be your bodyguard. Bodyguard for always."

Ronan saw hope flicker behind her fear, but the fear was still strong. "Can I think about it?"

"Think as much as you want." Ronan leaned to kiss her mouth, tasting coffee and the cinnamon Ellison had sprinkled onto it for her. "Accepting my mate-claim will protect you more, but I'll protect you no matter what."

Elizabeth kissed him in return, then she caressed his cheek, a touch that had already become dear to him. "Thank you, Ronan," she whispered.

*** *** ***

Scott was indeed full of chagrin when he woke in the morning, and very hung over from the effects of his Collar. The whole family took pity on him, and Ronan made his favorite breakfast, a mountain of waffles with berries and honey.

Scott then said that Elizabeth and Mabel wouldn't have to move; he'd go. He'd already called Spike and arranged to stay with Spike and his grandmother, both well capable of keeping Scott in line. Scott left after breakfast, mumbling about bunking down with crazy-ass wildcats, but he seemed relieved to go.

Mabel was happy to stay longer with Cherie, and now she was talking about coloring her hair to match Cherie's natural brown and blond chunks.

Elizabeth opened the store with Ronan, Ellison and Spike showing up to continue fixing the wall and door. Elizabeth felt a little shy with Ronan after the declarations of the night before, but Ronan took it all in stride, remaining his normal, bantering self. He never mentioned the mate-claim or the secret of her past Elizabeth had revealed to him.

He was giving her space, she realized. No man Elizabeth had gone out with had given her time to think things over. Elizabeth thought she could fall in love with Ronan for that alone.

Over the next few days, her life took on a new and comfortable routine. She and Ronan rode together to the store every morning, Spike and Ellison showing up to work on finishing and painting the new wall and door. When that was done, they looked around for other things to fix. They charged her nothing, behaving as though repairing her shop was what they woke up every day to do. Elizabeth knew that other Shifters — the trackers, everyone called them — lingered nearby to guard the store and look out for cops, but Elizabeth never saw them.

Rebecca's birthday fell on that Wednesday. As much as Ronan claimed she didn't want to be reminded, Rebecca was pleased and touched when Ronan made her a special breakfast Wednesday morning, and the family plied her with cards and gifts. Rebecca opened the one from Ronan in trepidation, clearly expecting a joke, and then looked stunned at the artisan-crafted glass-bead jewelry Elizabeth had picked out for her. The colors were bold but beautiful, the artisan knowing how to combine shape and color for a pleasing whole. Rebecca kissed Ronan soundly on the cheek, although she thanked Elizabeth, knowing the choice had been hers.

Pablo Marquez did not return that week, nor did he send anyone in his stead to make threats. The neighborhood around Elizabeth's store and house remained quiet. Elizabeth started to hope that she could go home soon.

Then again, she was not all that eager to run back to the lonely house she and Mabel occupied. The house could be lively when Mabel was there with her joie de vivre, but Mabel would start back to college in a week or so, and between that, the shop, and her many friends, Mabel would rarely be home. Elizabeth suspected that, anytime now, Mabel would announce plans to move out on her own. And then Elizabeth would be alone again.

Ronan's house, on the other hand, was full of life. When Elizabeth went home, she'd miss the loveable Olaf, Rebecca's wisecracks about anything and everything, Cherie's young enthusiasm, Ronan's giant breakfasts, and of course, Ronan himself.

Every night after Elizabeth closed the store, she went with him to Liam's bar. There she'd talk and joke with Andrea, Glory, Ellison, and other Shifters she was coming to know. Whenever Ronan took a break, he'd sit down with Elizabeth, and at the end of the night, they rode home on Ronan's bike, Elizabeth's arms around his waist.

And they'd talk. Morning, noon, and night, she and Ronan seemed to never run out of conversation, or jokes about anything they could think of. Even silences with him were companionable, Elizabeth never feeling pressured to come up with something brilliant to say.

She'd never had a relationship like this, where she could actually *talk* to a guy. What's more, Ronan listened. It was a new sensation. In Elizabeth's previous relationships, the man in question had expected her to talk when he wanted her to, shut up when he wanted her to, and have sex with him whenever he wanted her to. Whenever *he* wanted, never mind Elizabeth's needs. His pleasure counted, not hers.

Ronan, on the other hand, was perfectly happy to steal kisses with her, as though they were wayward teenagers, whenever and wherever she liked. They made a game of it, coming up with unlikely and unusual places to duck away for kissing: her office bathroom, the broom closet at the bar, behind the back shelves in her store, in the root cellar of Ronan's house, in the back of Ellison's pickup. The Shifters—especially Rebecca and Ellison—made fun of them, but Ronan lapped up their teasing with enjoyment.

Elizabeth liked the turn her life had taken, which at the same time seemed fragile and new, like a seedling lifting a first tender shoot above the soil. There was hope and warmth, but also fear of impending storms.

The next storm came in the form of Julio Marquez, who was waiting for them in the shadows of the Shifter bar's parking lot when Ronan and Elizabeth emerged the next Friday night. The bar had closed an hour before, Ronan shutting down for Liam so Liam could go home to his family.

Ronan stepped fully in front of Elizabeth. Nate and Spike came out of the darkness to flank Julio, Nate in his human form, Spike as a jaguar.

Julio opened his hands then carefully lifted his jacket to show that he carried no weapon. His face sported healing cuts from his fight with Ronan, reminders of Ronan's strength, but also reminders that Ronan could temper his strength.

"I came alone," Julio said. "I just want to talk to you."

One week ago, Elizabeth had grown dizzy with terror when she'd looked into Julio's cold eyes over his gun. Now she tasted pure anger. A spark from Ronan's Collar flashed white in the night, and he growled.

Julio raised his hands. "I swear to God, I only want to talk. You made a fool out of me, *chica*, but I'm not crazy enough to go one-on-one with a Shifter."

Elizabeth stood in silence. Anything she said—even agreeing to let Julio speak his piece—might allow his lawyer to claim that her testimony against him was compromised. She was willing to bet that any lawyer hired by the Marquez brothers would be slippery enough to do so.

"You have three seconds to leave," Ronan said to Julio. "Or I go through you."

"No, no." Julio took a step back. "I'm here to apologize. My brother was right—I was stupid."

Elizabeth remained silent, and Ronan followed her lead.

Julio went on. "I know you think I've come here to ask you not to testify against me. And you're right. I really don't want to go to prison. I'm sorry for what I did, but I was just having fun. You know, showing off for my friends."

He was a cool little liar. He might dupe a person more naive than Elizabeth, but she'd seen many performances like his, most of them better. Julio had been ready to kill her last Friday night, not caring who she was or who in the world depended on her. She'd been a means to get to the money, something to be disposed afterward. That was all.

"I know you're pissed off at me," Julio said. "So I'll make a deal with you. You know the Shifter fight clubs?"

Ronan waited. He was a frightening sight out here in the dark, looming like a giant, his Collar gleaming in the moonlight.

"Here's my deal," Julio said. "You, Shifter, come out to the fight club out east of here tomorrow night and fight my champion. Spike knows where it is. My champion's a good fighter, but I've seen you, and I think you'd have a chance against him. You win, I leave you and your lady alone forever. You testify at my trial, do whatever you want. If my champion wins then you agree to not to testify, get out of town, and leave me the hell alone. Got it?"

Elizabeth longed to shout at him, to lambaste him for coming here and expecting her to cut a deal, when he'd been the one who'd shoved a pistol into her face and tried to take away everything she had. What should she do, apologize for not being a helpless victim? She clamped her lips closed, struggling against the words.

Ronan's Collar sparked again. "Not interested," he said.

He started walking, directly at Julio. Julio sidestepped, and Ronan pulled Elizabeth along past him. Nate and Spike closed in.

"You're going to want to take my deal," Julio called, voice edged with desperation. "Don't walk away from me so fast . . . *Rachel*."

Elizabeth knew she shouldn't stop, shouldn't react. She should ignore him, have every inch of her body language say, *Who's Rachel?*

But she froze, one foot in the act of striding, while fear hit her so hard she wanted to be sick. She sensed Ronan slow beside her, felt his curiosity, his caution.

"Rachel Sullivan," Julio went on, glee in his voice. "You have a juvey record longer than mine. Yeah, I can see what's in old files. My brother got into bed with a hacker — literally, she's screwing him. Mouthy bitch, but she knows her stuff. You got mixed up with a very, very bad dude, didn't you? I bet he'd love to have Pablo call him and tell him he knows where Rachel Sullivan is."

Ronan's growls rose as he spun around, his Collar throwing out sparks like lightning. Nate and Spike flanked him.

Julio backed away, but he didn't run. "Kill me now, and an email gets sent to his phone in the morning. If you agree, and I make it home before the message is timed to send, I'll erase it. You say no, or you kill me . . . well, there will be no one to push the delete key. Then you have to deal with *him*."

Elizabeth finally spoke. "I take it your brother doesn't know about this little deal?"

"Pablo told me to take care of my problems on my own. So I'm taking care of them. But my brother and his hacker chick know all about you and your sister. The foster homes, your arrests for pick-pocketing and shoplifting and your little scams, you avoiding jail by the skin of your teeth."

"I never went down for armed robbery," Elizabeth said, voice tight.

"You would have, eventually. You were a desperate little *chiquita*."

"You aren't desperate," Elizabeth snapped.

"I told you. I did it for fun. Well, Shifter? You gonna show up and fight? Or let your *punta*'s ex find her and let her know how pissed he is at her for leaving him? Probably he'll show you too."

"No, Ronan," Elizabeth said. "Don't bargain with him."

Ronan's voice cut over hers. "Get the hell out of here, you little shit, before I let Spike rip you apart."

"Take my offer, Bear," Julio said, stepping backward toward the darkness. "Take it or that email goes."

"Fine. Spike."

Spike rushed him. Julio turned and ran, satisfactorily fast, but he called back, "See you tomorrow night!"

He melted into the darkness, a kid well versed in getting away as quickly as he could. Spike loped after him and Nate followed.

Ronan watched them go, remaining planted until he was well out of sight. He took Elizabeth's hand again. "Come on. Let's go home."

Elizabeth ripped herself out of his grasp. "Don't you dare say *let's go home* like nothing's wrong."

"Let's go home and talk about it, inside," Ronan said emphatically.

"Yes, all right." She was shaking. Hearing her real name come out of Julio's mouth had made bile rise in her throat. "You can't seriously mean you'll do what he wants."

"I don't," Ronan said. He leaned to her. "Now, *let's go home.*"

\*\*\* \*\*\* \*\*\*

Elizabeth held it together long enough to ride behind Ronan through the streets of Shiftertown to his house tucked beneath spreading trees. Ronan drove around to the back of the house and shut off the bike. No lights glowed in the house and they didn't have outdoor lights to illuminate the back— Shifters saw well in the dark.

Ronan lifted off his helmet and hung it on the bike, and did the same with Elizabeth's. Before she could move toward the house, he put large hands on her shoulders and turned her to face him.

"Tell me the guy's name."

"Not if you mean you'll go after him. He's too dangerous, Ronan. If you think Pablo Marquez is dangerous, he's small potatoes compared to this man."

"I know he's dangerous, and I know Marquez is too. I told Julio I'd agree to the fight so he wouldn't send the damn email. Julio's a brat, but he can hurt you just by being stupid. Tell me his name. We need to know."

"What is wrong with you?" Elizabeth's voice rose, and she didn't care. "You Shifters think you're unstoppable. Well, you're not. You wear Collars, for God's sake. You have to live in Shiftertowns, you're treated like second-class citizens. What makes you think you can go after a huge drug lord and survive when the cops, the FBI, and even other gangs can't make a dent?"

"Because Shifters don't give a rat's ass about Collars and Shiftertowns and idiotic human rules!"

Ronan shouted back. "The humans feel so good that they've restricted us and controlled us, don't they? So safe, because the beasts are in the cage. Meanwhile, if you hadn't noticed, we do whatever the hell we want."

Yes, Elizabeth had noticed that. She remembered the courtroom, where the judge, prosecutor, and bailiff had been nervous and ill at ease, while Liam and Ronan hadn't been worried at all. They'd been in control, and they'd known it. Ronan, also, nonchalantly escorted Elizabeth to her store every morning, blatantly disregarding his restriction to remain in Shiftertown. He took precautions not to be caught, but he went.

"I still don't want you fighting whoever Julio's coerced into working for him," Elizabeth said.

The glint in Ronan's eye was maddening. "Why not? It might be fun."

"*Ronan*."

"You let me worry about the fight, and you let me worry about this drug lord. Now, who is he?"

"Damn it, Ronan, if you go up against him, he'll kill you. He won't wait to talk. He'll kill you and all your Shifter friends. I'm not kidding."

"I'm not kidding, either. Why do you think Pablo Marquez has left you alone all week? Because Dylan and Sean went and had a little talk with him. Marquez is making plans to shut down his business here and open up somewhere else."

"I never heard that."

"Of course you didn't. The Morrisseys, they do their shit, and they shut up about it. I didn't tell you, because I liked seeing you not worry about him. Now I want to make sure you never have to worry about this other guy — whose name you're about to give me."

Elizabeth pressed her hands together. She didn't know what to do, and her indecision and fear made her eyes blur with tears.

Ronan softened his touch. "Sweetheart," he said in the tender tone she'd come to love. He drew her against him. "Don't be scared. I take care of you now. That's what it means to be mate-claimed."

"But I could lose you." Her voice broke. "I finally found something good, and I'll *lose you!*"

Ronan cuddled her close. "Lizzie-girl," he said, lips brushing her hair. "Shh."

They stood together in the night breeze that cooled the humid air, rocking together. The pain that laced Elizabeth's heart made more tears spill to wet the black T-shirt stretched over Ronan's chest. She'd had so few good things in her life, so few good people, that everything in her cried, *Don't let go.*

She wiped tears from her eyes as she rose on her tiptoes and kissed him.

Ronan's mouth was a warm place in the night, tasting of heat and spice. Elizabeth clung to him as he kissed her back, his tongue stroking hers with gentle possession.

This man had become, even in such a short time, a rock in her life. To have someone take him away from her — *no!*

Ronan warmed her back with his big hands, his touch soothing. "We should get inside," he said. "Not the house. Rebecca's upstairs taking care of Olaf, and your sister and Cherie are talking like crazy in your room. Shifter hearing. And scent," he said, by way of explanation as to how he knew this. "Besides, my room's always a mess."

He gave her a little shamefaced smile as he said this last, which made Elizabeth kiss him again. He gestured toward the Den, and she nodded. Ronan took her hand and led her there.

# Chapter Thirteen

The Den was empty, dark, and quiet. Ronan turned on a lamp and closed the shades against the night.

He didn't try anything romantic like carrying Elizabeth to the bed this time. He simply kissed her while he slid his hands under the hem of her cropped top and lifted it off over her head.

She wore a tiny black bra underneath, a strip of satin and lace above which her breasts swelled. She closed her eyes as Ronan drew his fingertip along her butterfly tattoo, bared in its entirety now. It had tasted fine the other night. Ronan lowered his head to taste it again.

Elizabeth made a little noise of pleasure, and her fingers came up to furrow his hair. She smelled good, the cinnamon scent overlaid with her own musk. He tasted perspiration and *her* as he glided his tongue over the smooth line of her tattoo.

Elizabeth slid her hands down his back and tugged at his T-shirt. Ronan obliged her by pulling off the shirt and tossing it away. He was rewarded by Elizabeth running her hands down his torso, fingers finding his flat nipples among wiry hair.

"You have to be the largest man I've ever seen," she said.

"Kodiaks get big." Ronan slid his hands to her waist. "You, though, are tiny."

She laughed softly. "Oh, please, I've never been called *tiny* in my life."

"You are to me. And yet . . ." He moved his hands beneath her breasts. "You have curves a man could lose himself in."

"You aren't bad yourself." Elizabeth skimmed her hands down to his buttocks, which were still cupped by his jeans. She usually liked to hook her fingers through his belt loops, but this time, she slid them into his back pockets.

"I could grow to like this," Ronan said. "But I'm getting a little frenzied."

"The frenzy again?"

Ronan snaked his thumbs under the elastic of her bra, finding a soft cushion of woman beneath. "A Shifter's curse, the mating frenzy. When it comes upon us, we'll do anything to hole up with our mates and not come out until it's over. For days. Or weeks."

"Good."

Ronan warmed. "Good?"

"Means you'll be too busy to go to that stupid fight club."

"Maybe." Ronan's blood was hot with need, his skin starting to bead with sweat. Elizabeth was lovely, and soft, and damn sexy in that bra. Choosing between lying with her for a week or fighting a smelly Shifter wasn't difficult. Ronan ran his fingers around to the back of her bra and fumbled with the hooks. "I'm not good at this."

Her smile made her eyes soft. "Don't tell me you're inexperienced."

"I've never been with a human woman, no." Ronan finally worked the two catches free. "I think I've been missing out."

Elizabeth took her hands from Ronan's pockets and slid the bra straps from her shoulders. Her breasts came into view, round and full, tips dusky. She had another tattoo, he discovered, a tiny one just below her left nipple—a perfectly formed little fairy with finely penned wings. He lowered his head and kissed it.

Elizabeth's intake of breath made him warmer still, and he licked where he'd kissed.

"That hurt when I got it done," Elizabeth said in a near-whisper. "I thought I was crazy. The lady who did it for me, though, she was a real artist."

"I like it," Ronan said into her skin. He moved his mouth upward and caught her areola with his tongue.

Elizabeth stood perfectly still, sensations pouring through her as his mouth did its dance. Her body was open and hot, the space between her legs relaxed and wanting him.

She unhooked his belt and pulled it open then popped the button of his jeans. Ronan came up, his eyes holding the same longing she felt. He quickly pulled off his boots then unzipped and got rid of the jeans, pulling his underwear down with them.

Elizabeth had seen him naked before, but this time was different. Before, he'd been shifting, a warrior, protecting her. Now he was a man, bared to take her to bed.

She ran her hands down his chest, over his flat abdomen, and stopped when she reached the hardness of him. Elizabeth became needier still as she closed her hands around it.

"So the rumors are true," she said. "About the extra inches."

"Every single one of them, sweetheart."

She wanted to laugh. "You're full of yourself."

"No, you are full of myself."

"Shithead."

Elizabeth rose on her tiptoes, still holding on, and kissed his mouth. Ronan made a noise of enjoyment as she squeezed him, and his answering kiss took her breath away.

No more holding back. Ronan yanked open her jeans, the top button flying across the room. Before Elizabeth could move to assist, he had the jeans down, hands deftly removing her high-heeled half-boots at the same time. Next came her black satin panties that matched her bra, his large hands warming her legs.

Now she was bare, and so was he, standing body to body. He kissed her as he scooped her against him, lifted her, and carried her to the bed.

He stripped back the quilts, laying her on the sheets before he climbed into bed beside her. Elizabeth slid her hand again to his very erect shaft, knowing exactly what she wanted to do. She came up on her knees and coaxed him onto his back, then she straddled him, sitting back on his shins so she could keep rubbing him with her hand.

Ronan curled his arms behind his head, watching her with intense eyes while she stroked him. She could tell he was holding back, keeping himself from reaching for her, while waiting to see what she'd do.

"Lizzie-girl," he said, voice raw. "You're going to kill me."

Elizabeth gave him a sly look. She leaned down and licked his navel, then let her tongue glide down, all the way down. She traveled the length of him and closed her mouth over his tip.

Not for long. Ronan growled, a sound that came from the depths of him. He dragged Elizabeth up and over onto her back, cradling her the whole time so she came down softly on the mattress. He parted her thighs with one large knee, and then he was over her, the strong shaft she'd stroked sliding into her.

Elizabeth arched her body, rising to meet him. He pushed inside smoothly, she so slick for him, that it was nothing but astonishing pleasure.

Ronan's eyes flickered, becoming the lighter color Shifters' eyes seemed to go when they wanted to change. But he didn't shift. He filled her, his muscles moving as he kept his weight from crushing her, even now fearing to hurt her.

Elizabeth hooked one leg around him, gliding her foot up to his firm buttocks. Ronan kissed her as he loved her, hot, needy kisses. She tasted his loneliness and his longing, his hope that perhaps his loneliness was at an end.

At times in the past, when Elizabeth had lain with a man, she'd felt alone and disconnected, even in the middle of sex. With Ronan, she was connected, not just physically, but with a warmth that ran through her heart and through her blood.

She whispered his name, and he looked into her eyes, far gone in feeling. Elizabeth's body opened to his, and the same feeling came to her. They were whole, joined, like two streams of fire that ran together to become one.

And then Elizabeth's thoughts dissolved into pure feeling. The intensity of them crashed over her, erasing fear, pain, isolation . . . everything gone. She was with Ronan, shielded from the world, from everything but this joy.

She rose to her climax on a wash of white-hot pleasure, hearing her voice ring out, Ronan's joining it. They rippled together, Ronan riding her, his kisses hot and primal.

They loved for a long, long time, until manic heat slowed to loving warmth. They fell back to the bed, mouths meeting, hands moving, each taking and giving, until all was quiet, and they drowsed together on the rumpled sheets.

*** *** ***

A long time later, Elizabeth pried open heavy eyes to see Ronan sitting on the edge of the bed, staring at something in his hand. No, he was tapping something, which glowed. Elizabeth rubbed her eyes and saw that he held a phone.

"You're going through my pockets now?" she asked.

"This was on the floor." Ronan moved his thumb to scroll through lists of phone numbers. "Must have fallen out when we were ripping off each other's clothes. But this isn't your phone."

"I know that." Elizabeth traced the arcs of the Celtic tattoo on his back. "It's Julio Marquez's."

Ronan looked back and down at her, his eyes shining in the garish light from the phone. "And you have it, because . . ."

"I lifted it when we went by him in the parking lot. I thought it might be useful." She lay down again, keeping her fingertips on Ronan's back. "No, to be honest, I was being a pain in the ass. My way of spitting at him."

"I think you're right though — this will be useful," Ronan said. "Very. Julio makes a lot of phone calls. Most recently to someone named . . . Casey."

Elizabeth froze, her blood like ice. "Zach Casey," she whispered.

Ronan turned all the way around, getting on the bed with her again. "The guy you ran away from?"

"I told you, Ronan. Please." She closed her hand around his arm, feeling her fears pour over her. "Don't go near him. I think I'd die if I lost you."

Ronan clicked off the phone and laid it on the nightstand. "It looks like our friend Julio already called him. I'll make three guesses what he talked about."

"Damn him. Why can't he leave me alone?" Elizabeth wasn't sure if she meant Marquez or Zach, but it didn't much matter.

"He will," Ronan said. His voice held none of its usual banter, the humor he hid behind. "I'm willing to bet that this fight is Julio's dastardly plan to get back at you and at me. So I'm going to spring his little trap and bring along some secret weapons of my own. And I'll need your help, so don't come over all damsel in distress on me."

"I'm not scared for me; I'm scared for you," Elizabeth said.

Ronan went on, unworried. "I need to talk to Spike, and I need to talk to Sean. And I promise you, Lizzie-girl, after tomorrow, you won't need to be afraid anymore. Of anyone." He kissed her, the heat of their lovemaking lingering in him. "Do this with me?"

Elizabeth scrubbed her hand through her hair, making the red-streaked chunks stick out. "Goldilocks was pretty resilient, I guess."

"I heard she shacked up with the papa bear, and they lived happily ever after."

Elizabeth frowned. "I don't remember that version of the story."

"How about we discuss it? Sean's probably still up, but I hate to disturb his mate by calling him now. He'll wait."

"Discuss it how?" Elizabeth's fears didn't go away, but a pleasant warmth made them recede a little. She was safe from Zach Casey in Shiftertown, no matter what Zach or Julio might think.

"How about we bag the discussion?" Ronan put his hand on her waist and half rolled onto her, warming her like the best of blankets.

"Sounds good to me," Elizabeth said, and all conversation ceased.

*** *** ***

Saturday was the busiest for Elizabeth's store. Ronan wanted her to stay in Shiftertown, but Elizabeth refused to hide and miss her best sales day of the week. They were warned now to look out for Zach, she said, and again, she wasn't going to let fear ruin her life.

Ronan scented Elizabeth's adrenaline running high as she opened the store, but only innocuous human customers came into the store, followed by Glory and Rebecca, who took a long time over their shopping. Elizabeth knew she was being babysat, but she said nothing about it.

Spike and Sean came in through the back to speak to Ronan, but no one was doing any carpentry today.

"Sure, I can get you into the Shifter fights," Spike said to Ronan. They stood in Elizabeth's office, door closed, Elizabeth out front with her customers and Glory and Rebecca. "Everyone likes fresh blood. But I never heard about a champion sponsored by Marquez. He can't be local. Did you get his name?"

"Julio didn't say." Ronan leaned on the desk and thought of Elizabeth curled against him in the night, her body fitting so well with his.

"Not good," Spike said. "You gotta watch yourself in these places, Ronan. The only rules are that you stay inside the ring and don't use a weapon. Other than that, anything goes. It's Shifters letting out their wild."

"You think I can't be a little wild?" Ronan asked with a mild grin.

"I think you haven't been in a long time. Escorting drunk humans out of the bar is different from going up against a tiger-wildcat who eats raw steak for breakfast and is dying for a fight."

"I bet he could win with just his breath," Ronan said. Sean chuckled.

"Take it seriously, Ronan. These guys are seasoned. If Marquez has a champion, it means he's won a good share of the fights. He won't be a walkover."

"I've watched a couple of these matches," Sean said. "I believe him."

"It's not to the death though, right?" Ronan asked. "I don't want to be killing a guy with a mate and cubs who need him."

Spike shook his head. "Not to the death. We all want to go home afterward. The refs call it when a Shifter can't get up again. But things can get pretty bad." He looked at Sean. "I don't think you should go at all, Sean. A Guardian will make people nervous."

"Marquez also might decide that a fight to the death is what he wants," Sean said. "What if one of them pegs it, and there's no Guardian handy?"

Spike looked uneasy, but Ronan thought he knew why. Not because Sean might be needed, but Sean might tell Liam about Spike doing the fights. And no one wanted to piss off Liam.

"Don't worry," Sean said to him. "I'll be incognito, and I won't tell my brother."

Elizabeth's voice came from the doorway. "I thought you'd come here to talk him out of it, Sean."

All three of them jumped like guilty teenagers as Elizabeth walked into the room.

She was unhappy, that was obvious, but Ronan took in her jeans and tight red top, her high-heeled half-boots, the streaks in her hair that matched her shirt, and felt his mating frenzy stir. The lines of the butterfly peeping over the top's neckline reminded him of the beautiful little fairy on her breast. For a moment, whatever Sean was saying went fuzzy.

"I'm here to help you in a different way, lass," he thought Sean said. "With me trusty laptop." He'd set it up on Elizabeth's desk. The laptop looked plain, low-end, but Sean's fingers skimmed the keyboard, and screens began to pop up under his touch. "You're going to tell me everything about Rachel Sullivan and her little sister, and they'll go away, forever." He wriggled his fingers a few inches above the keys. "Like magic."

"Forever." Elizabeth stared at the laptop, a strange expression on her face.

"No one will ever connect you with her again," Sean said. "And no one will be able to track you from that name — or that name from your current one. You'll have been Elizabeth Chapman from birth. Is that who you want to be?"

Elizabeth stilled, staring at the laptop as though it would leap from the table and devour her. Her need for touch, for reassurance, screamed itself at Ronan.

But Ronan made himself stay where he was, though he had to clamp his arms across his middle to keep himself from going to her. She had to make this decision on her own, uninfluenced by Ronan, or Sean, or Julio, or Zach Casey.

Elizabeth drew a long breath, gaze flicking from the laptop to Ronan.

"Yes," she said.

*** *** ***

Elizabeth heard Ronan follow her out into the alley, where she'd gone to calm herself, to try to master her sudden dizziness. Inside, Sean was erasing — somehow — all trace of who Elizabeth used to be.

Ronan stopped beside her, leaning broad shoulders back against the wall, resting his booted foot against it. He said nothing and didn't reach for her. The man knew how to comfort simply by standing there.

"How can what Sean's doing help?" Elizabeth asked. "No matter how careful I was, Pablo Marquez's girlfriend found me out. How can Sean stop someone else from putting together the same information?"

"Because no hacker can out-hack a Guardian," Ronan said in a low voice. "Don't ask me how they do it. It's a secret known only to Guardians, and I'm not one, thank the Goddess."

"Why should he do this for me? If he's caught . . ." Elizabeth said the last in a murmur, glancing at the other closed doors in the alley.

"Sean, caught? You'd be amazed at what he and Liam get up to. Not to mention their dad."

"I don't want you going tonight, Ronan. I heard what Spike said." She looked up at him, big as a wrestler, no softness about him. "But you're not going to listen to me, are you?"

"Oh, I'm listening, Lizzie-girl."

"But you'll do it anyway."

"It's a good chance to get Marquez and his threats out of your life. Sean can help you with his laptop, me with my fists." He slanted her a look that made her remember his warmth in the night and the way she'd felt safe in his arms. "I'm pretty damn good at what I do."

He was, though she knew he didn't mean sex. "You're not even supposed to leave Shiftertown," she said, still in the low murmur. "Let alone go to some barn in the middle of nowhere."

"Even more of a challenge."

She let out an exasperated sigh. "I'm grateful for what Sean's doing, but erasing my info won't hide me from Zach. Julio's already contacted him."

"Elizabeth." Ronan faced her, resting his hands on the wall on either side of her. "You never have to worry about the Marquez brothers, or this Zach, or anything they might do to you, again. Whatever they do, it won't touch you. We've got your back."

No one but Ronan had ever said that to her and meant it. Ronan's eyes held nothing but sincerity, his vast strength like a barrier between her and the world.

"Why would you all do this for me? A week and a half ago, you barely knew me."

Ronan leaned closer. She'd never be able to duck away from him before he could close his arms around her, and she didn't particularly want to.

"I mate-claimed you," Ronan said. "That makes you one of us. You might walk away later, and we'll let you, but we won't let anything happen to you. You've become an honorary member of my clan, of Ellison's pack, of Sean and Liam's pride . . . until you become a full member of my clan." He came closer still and nuzzled her. "I'm hoping that happens soon."

"No pressure," she said, but she smiled.

"Nope." He nuzzled her again and kissed her softly. "No pressure at all."

"I'm coming with you tonight," she said.

"Well, yeah, I hope so. Wouldn't be the same without my mate-to-be cheering me on."

"Who says I'll cheer, Bear with Large Ego?"

"You will. And when I win, you'll be all over me."

"In your dreams."

"Oh, yeah," Ronan said. "And sweetie, trust me, I have some great dreams."

# Chapter Fourteen

The makeshift arena for the Shifter fights was at the end of a dirt road a long way north and east of the 290. Elizabeth hung onto Ronan as he guided his bike down an FM road, then a county road, and finally an unmarked road where the pavement ended after only a few feet.

At the end of this dirt trail was an abandoned farm tucked among bushy trees, ponds and stock tanks shimmering in the moonlight. The barn was an incredibly long metal building, rusting now, built to store hay for a ton of cattle.

The hay was long gone, along with the livestock that had eaten it. Now the barn smelled rusty, musty, and muddy. But tonight, with fires blazing in barrels up and down its center, it was alive with animation and excitement.

Elizabeth tasted the anticipation as she walked in close behind Ronan. Behind her came Spike, wearing a muscle shirt that showed off his completely inked arms. He had beautiful tattoos, drawn by a true artist, colors bright and flowing. Ellison came behind him, in his usual cowboy boots, black button-down shirt, and Stetson.

Sean walked behind Ellison, minus his sword. But though he claimed he'd come "incognito," everyone recognized Sean. Elizabeth saw the Shifters back away as he walked by, the Shifters uneasy. Andrea had told Elizabeth that while Shifters respected Guardians, Guardians were reminders of death, which didn't sit well with them. Sean took it in stride, but Elizabeth had noticed the quietness in him, and how he drank in Andrea's love for him like a man who'd gone thirsty too long.

Andrea had stayed home because of her advanced pregnancy, but plenty of women mixed in with the crowd of males. Several of the females were tall Shifter women, but most were human. Shifter groupies were there, both men and women. Some wore fake wildcat or wolf ears, others had painted whiskers on their faces or made up their eyes to look feline. The female groupies wore scanty clothing; the males who wanted sex wore low-slung jeans and tight T-shirts or no shirts at all. The men who'd come simply to hang out with Shifters dressed more conservatively and eyed the female groupies — and some, the male groupies — with calculating stares.

The male humans took full notice of Elizabeth as she walked behind Ronan in her red top and jeans, gazes drifting to her tatt. Elizabeth had been sized up before, but never had she felt so much like a walking piece of meat. The Shifters were eyeing her too, she saw, but then they'd look at Ronan, look again at her, inhale, and slide their gazes away.

Not all of these Shifters were from Ronan's Shiftertown, she understood. The fight clubs drew Shifters from Shiftertowns in Austin, Hill Country, San Antonio, and from as far away as Houston to the east, Waco to the north, and San Angelo to the west. Humans did not like Shifters from different Shiftertowns mingling, but fight clubs had become a melting pot, according to Spike. And, the tattooed Shifter added, what humans didn't know wouldn't hurt Shifters.

The barn had been divided into thirds, plenty of room for three fights to take place simultaneously. A fight had already commenced in the far end, Shifters and humans alike shouting encouragement.

By the time Ronan and Elizabeth reached the last ring, the two Shifters, a wolf and a wildcat, were all over each other. The wildcat had a lot of lion in it, mane and all, but the wolf was just big. The wolf's Collar snapped and sparked, though the wildcat's remained strangely silent.

"Shit," Sean said behind her. "That's my dad."

The wildcat was winning. The wolf snarled and fought, its Collar going crazy. The wildcat finally got a large paw around the wolf and slammed it to the ground. The wildcat held the wolf there, the wolf's eyes white with rage and pain.

Five Shifter men leapt over the low circle of cinderblocks that marked out the ring, shouting and making waving motions with their arms. The referees, Elizabeth guessed. Ending the fight.

The wildcat backed away. The wolf rolled to its feet, shaking its body like a dog. The wolf's shape undulated as it shook, ending with the wolf becoming a young man with shaggy black hair. The young man rose upright and put his hands on his hips, breathing hard, Collar still sparking.

The wildcat morphed into the tall form of Dylan Morrissey. Ronan had told Elizabeth that Dylan was aging even by Shifter standards, but in human terms Dylan looked like a man in his late forties at most, one in fantastic shape. His Collar was quiet, and he didn't seem much the worse for wear.

The refs called Dylan the winner, and those who'd bet in his favor went crazy.

"Dad!" Sean called.

Dylan saw them, stepped over the cinderblocks, and came to them, completely unworried that he was naked in front of Elizabeth. But many of the Shifters were already naked, stretching, warming up, getting ready for their bouts.

"Since when do you take part in Shifter fights?" Sean asked him.

Dylan shrugged. "They keep me on my toes."

"Does Liam know?"

Dylan took a shirt from Glory, who'd materialized out of the crowd. "Not everything I do is Liam's business, son."

Glory hung on Dylan's shoulder. "You got that right. Dylan fighting is damn sexy. Gets my blood pumping."

Sean looked embarrassed. Glory gave Elizabeth a thumb's up behind Dylan's back. Dylan turned away, as though uncaring what anyone thought of him, and Glory followed him into the crowd.

"Parents, eh?" Sean said to Elizabeth. "But what can I do? I'm glad Glory's only me step-mum."

"Treasure it, Sean," Elizabeth said over the noise. "I never had a dad, embarrassing or otherwise."

Sean gave her a nod. "You have a point. Liam and I lost our mum a long time ago."

Elizabeth touched his shoulder in sympathy, then she stopped. "Wait a sec. Why didn't Dylan's Collar go off?" She remembered Kim standing proudly in the courtroom, proclaiming that Ronan's Collar remaining dark meant he hadn't intended to hurt anyone. "They were fighting pretty hard. It didn't look like your dad was holding back in there."

Sean's gaze flicked from hers. "Could be lots of reasons."

Elizabeth recognized evasiveness when she heard and saw it. Apparently information about the Collars was need-to-know.

"Come on," Sean said, pretending he'd answered the question to her satisfaction. "Ronan's spotted Marquez."

Sean pushed through the crowd that waited for the next fight, and Elizabeth followed in his wake. Behind her, women were shouting for the next two heading into the ring. She also heard females she passed going crazy for Spike. They screamed his name or "There-he-is-oh-my-God-that's-*him!*"

Julio Marquez stood in a relatively empty space with three men around him, all human. No guns were visible, Shifters stationed at the entrance to check for them. No weapons were allowed inside the barn. There was no sign of Zach, either, though every tracker Liam employed was searching for him or here keeping a lookout for him.

"You showed up," Julio was saying when Elizabeth reached Ronan. "Good start. You should have left the *chica* at home, though."

Ronan ignored him. "So where's this champion?"

"You'll see him when you fight him. Half an hour. Ring two." He laughed. "Maybe it is a good thing you brought your bitch. She'll be on hand when you need to say good-bye."

Ronan turned away, his body language all that was contempt.

"He's up to something," Elizabeth said to him. "I mean more than trying to kill you and give me to Zach."

"Of course he's up to something," Ronan said. "He's a thief and a liar. It's just figuring out what and when." He slid his arm around Elizabeth's waist. "Half an hour, eh? Maybe he's right. Maybe I should take you into a corner and kiss you a while, just in case. We'll make Sean and Spike keep watch for us."

*** *** ***

Pablo Marquez was in the middle of a deal that could cinch him taking over the trade of the entire southern half of Texas. He could leave Austin and his sudden Shifter problem and hole up in a beautiful mansion by a lake. No more back alley body shops or too-curious neighbors in the suburbs. Solitude, a pool, and all the fine wine he could drink. He was becoming a connoisseur of the stuff.

The thin white man standing in front of him was one of the best smugglers in the business. But though the man knew how to move product, he needed someone on the street to sell it for him, and some of his Hill Country contacts had moved elsewhere. With banditry south of the border increasing, and enthusiastic vigilante border patrols keeping watch north of it, moving anything between the U.S. and Mexico, in either direction, was risky and expensive. But Pablo had the resources and connections, this man had the expertise, and they'd make beautiful money together. Pablo was going to land this.

Or so he thought, until his lieutenant's cell phone quietly rang and the man stepped into a corner to answer it. The lieutenant returned and whispered into Pablo's ear.

Pablo stopped. *Julio. Son of a . . .*

"Problem?" the smuggler said. He had a reedy voice but quiet strength behind it.

"No," Pablo said in a reassuring tone. "At least not for you." He gave him a wry look. "Family."

"Ah. I understand." The man's light blue gaze didn't waver. "Why don't you take care of that? I'll be back to talk later."

Which meant Pablo would probably never see him again. The smuggler wouldn't like any indication that Pablo's operation was the least bit unstable, which could equal said smuggler not getting paid. Even an unruly little brother could upset a touchy shipment. *Shit.*

But Pablo couldn't sit here and beg like a little girl for the man not to go. He nodded, pretending everything was cool. "Sure. You have my number. You let me know."

The man nodded. He held out a hand, and Pablo, his wrist still in a bandage, shook it.

The smuggler walked away, his thugs closing around him, and Pablo knew that was the last he'd see of him. He turned to his lieutenant. "Damn that little shit. Where did he take him? Where are they?"

*** *** ***

Ronan stripped off next to the middle ring half an hour later, but there was no sign of his opponent. Elizabeth held his clothes, hiding her nervousness. She was good at that, when she needed to be. Her courage made him warm with pride. Ronan's lips were a bit raw from kissing her outside, but he didn't mind. He hoped he'd have a chance to make them rawer later.

When the crowd parted to let through a large male Shifter, surrounded by Julio's bodyguards, Spike said behind Ronan, "Aw, crap."

"What?" Elizabeth asked. "What's wrong with him?"

So many things. First, the Shifter wasn't wearing a Collar. Second, the bodyguards weren't protecting the Shifter—they were keeping him penned so he wouldn't start fighting everyone he laid his bloodshot eyes on. Third, the man stank like holy hell.

"He's a feral," Ronan said.

"Feral?" Elizabeth's eyes widened. "What do you mean, *feral*?"

Spike answered. "It means his animal side is close to taking over." He wrinkled his once-broken nose. "The first thing to go is bathing."

"His animal side?" Elizabeth asked. "Because he's not wearing a Collar?"

"Anyone can go feral, with or without a Collar," Ronan said. "But it's harder with a Collar, because it tends to shock sense into you."

"We lived for centuries without Collars," Sean said, sounding grim. "And we never needed them to keep us tame. Seems nowadays, though, that most of the Shifters who refused to take the Collar are feral or heading that way."

"Great," Elizabeth said. "So not only is he feral, but he's angry because other Shifters let themselves be Collared?"

"She's got it," Spike said.

"Ronan, you can't fight him," Elizabeth said quickly. "Without a Collar, he has all the advantage."

"Too late," Ronan said. He touched her face and gave her one last, firm kiss. "I've fought ferals before, Lizzie. I can do this. This is my job."

Elizabeth looked up at him, eyes luminous, but she closed her mouth and nodded. Her expression told him, however, that she'd prefer to knock him on the head and drag him back home, and would have if she'd been able.

Shifter fights had few rules, Spike had said. Shifters could fight in whatever form they wanted, and shift back and forth during the fight if they felt like it. The only hard and fast rules were: no weapons of any kind—they couldn't hold anything at all, in fact; the fighters had to stay within the circle; and they had to fight, without rounds, until the refs decided that one Shifter was down so far it would be life-threatening for him to continue. The one who wasn't half-dead was declared the winner.

Ronan didn't recognize four of the five Shifters who stepped in to referee, but he rarely went to the other Shiftertowns in the area. He'd bet that Julio had instructed these refs to let the fight carry on past the point of no return.

Julio's bodyguards fell back, and the feral stepped into the ring. He rose to his full human height and fixed his red eyes on Ronan before he shifted.

The feral changed smoothly, almost effortlessly, and landed on all fours as a large Alaskan gray wolf.

The thing was huge. Ronan had met wolf Shifters in his area of Alaska, but he and the wolves had given each other a respectful distance. This wolf had lost respect for everything a long time ago.

Spike was spouting advice. "You can do this, Ronan. Don't try to take him down quickly—he's got the advantage of speed at the first, but you have the advantage of stamina. He'll wear down a long time before you will. Then you've got him."

Ronan nodded, but he had his own ideas. He stepped into the ring, staying human, and nodded to the refs that he was ready.

"What are you doing?" Elizabeth asked behind him. "Why don't you shift?"

"You can't talk to him once he's in the ring," he heard Spike say in the relative hush. "But you can yell for him all you want."

The quiet lasted another few seconds, then Elizabeth's shout sounded loud and clear.

*"Kick his ass, Ronan!"*

The crowd burst into sudden cacophony. Half the Shifters and groupies around them were taking the feral's side, or at least betting on him, but plenty shouted for Ronan. He was popular in the Austin Shiftertown.

Elizabeth's voice gave Ronan strength. She was the mate of his heart, and once he disposed of this effing feral and got rid of the rest of her problems, he would make her understand that.

Meanwhile, he stood, in his human form, and waited to see what the feral wolf would do.

The Lupine circled him, growling, hackles raised. Ronan turned with him, keeping his face to the wolf's.

The Lupine would try to goad Ronan into attacking first. But Ronan's Collar wouldn't go off as quickly if Ronan remained on the defensive. With any luck, Ronan could take down the Lupine before the Collar emitted more than a couple of sparks.

*Not gonna happen,* something inside him said. This was going to be a nasty, brutal fight, and Julio had known it would be.

He was aware of Sean, behind him, fading into the crowd. He and the rest of the trackers were here to keep tabs on Julio and find Casey, who must be around somewhere. Dylan being here wasn't a coincidence. Sean had not been surprised to find Dylan at the fights, but to find him actually fighting.

Ronan had planned to use the fight to distract Julio, but Julio was using the fight to distract Ronan. Ronan had to trust his friends now to take care of the periphery for him while he concentrated on the matter at hand.

Killing the feral.

Meanwhile, the feral was gearing up to kill Ronan.

*To the death? So be it.*

The Lupine suddenly launched himself straight at Ronan. Ronan opened his big arms and let him come.

The wolf landed against Ronan's chest, claws digging into human skin. Ronan endured it for the few seconds it took him to shift.

The Lupine now found himself inside the grip of a two-ton Kodiak bear.

The crowd went crazy. Ronan had told Elizabeth that he'd been nervous with all the Shifters watching him when he'd first come to Austin. Now he had to ignore a hundred Shifters surrounding him and shouting for blood. He made himself shut them out and focus on the wolf.

Ronan's strength was, well, his strength, and he used it to crush the feral between his huge paws. The Lupine twisted, and faster than Ronan could have guessed he'd be able to, tore himself out of Ronan's grasp. The Lupine landed on his feet, mouth open as he leapt for Ronan's throat.

Ronan roared, paws coming out to stop the leap, but the wolf moved like smoke to close on Ronan and sink his teeth into Ronan's neck. Ronan shook himself like a dog, but the Lupine held on, his body flopping.

The crowed shouted, and Elizabeth cried his name. The sound of her voice galvanized him. Ronan grabbed the wolf and yanked him away, feeling his own fur and flesh come away in the Lupine's teeth.

The wolf landed on all fours. Ronan rose up on his hind legs, roaring again, fur rising on his ruff, a Kodiak at his most intimidating.

Ronan came down and charged the wolf. Ronan's Collar sparked, but his fury didn't let him feel it. He went for the wolf, who suddenly wasn't in the spot he'd occupied a second ago.

The bastard could *move*. Ronan swung around. The wolf was waiting, but evidently thought Ronan's bulk would slow him more than it did. Ronan's blow caught him on the side of the head, even as the wolf danced aside.

The watchers roared. The noise swelled louder and louder, until Ronan could hear nothing but it and the crackling of his Collar. He ran at the wolf again, who was feinting and snapping. Ronan's animal was taking over, lust for the kill overcoming all reason, but the human part of him still felt the Collar.

*This is going to hurt like a bitch,* was Ronan's last coherent thought before he charged.

# Chapter Fifteen

Pablo Marquez heard the noise of the fighting long before he reached the barn at the top of the hill, the edgy roar of people in a blood frenzy.

He and his four bodyguards had had to park at the end of a long line of cars on the dirt road and hike up to the door of the huge barn. A massive number of people and Shifters crowded around one of the rings inside, no other fights going on.

A large Shifter stepped into his path. Pablo recognized him as one of the Shifters who'd come to the body shop, the black-haired one called Nate. "No weapons," Nate said. "You gotta leave your guns in your car."

Rules of the fight clubs. But the space between Pablo's shoulder blades was itching, a sign he'd always learned to heed. His instincts had saved his ass more than once. At the moment, they were telling him to keep his gun close at hand. "We're not going in," he said to Nate. "Just tell me who's fighting."

"A bear called Ronan, and a feral Lupine. Don't know his name."

Mother of God. What was Julio *doing*? "Stop the fight. The Lupine's mine."

Nate narrowed his eyes. "Shifters fight by their choice, not for someone else."

"Yeah, well, that Shifter's insane and doesn't know what he's doing. My brother's running him, and he has no right to. The Shifter belongs to me."

Nate didn't move, but Pablo felt the man's anger like a cold front. "No one owns a Shifter."

"My brother thinks he does. Stop the damn fight."

"It's against the rules."

"*Cristo*." Pablo started to say more, but he sensed, rather than saw, shadows under the trees to the left of the barn. He signaled his guards to follow and noticed, distractedly, that the Shifter faded back inside the barn, out of sight.

"Julio," Pablo said as he approached his younger brother. "What the hell do you think you're doing?"

His brother detached himself from a fairly large group of men, some Latino, some white. "Oh, good," Julio said. "I was hoping you'd come."

"*Idiota*. You cost me the biggest deal I was ever going make in this town. To do what? Run my Shifter and try to get back at that girl? Let it go. If you make me lose the bail money because you do something stupid, I will beat you until you can't stand."

"You're running scared from *Shifters*, man," Julio said, his voice filled with disgust. "You backed down from them. You let them do what they wanted."

"I didn't back down because I was scared, you shit. I've learned how to weigh risk with reward. The risks in this case are too great, and I'm not going to get a big reward going up against a bunch of Shifters."

"Whatever, man. It's another way to say you let them walk all over you. I think you aren't strong enough for this business. So I'm taking it."

"Don't be such a dumb-ass." Pablo glanced at the white man who had a big, shining Sig in a holster under his jacket. "Who the hell is this?"

Julio started to speak, but the man forestalled him. "The name's Casey. Zach Casey. I don't really give a damn which of you wins this family spat, but Julio says if he wins it, I get my girlfriend back. Thanks for finding her."

Pablo looked him up and down in impatience. Another person who couldn't cut their losses. Elizabeth Chapman, or Rachel Sullivan, whatever you wanted to call her, had left this S.O.B. six years ago. Move on, already.

Julio had his hand on his holster. "You were the dumb-ass to come out here, bro," he said to Pablo. "All I had to do was have one of Zach's crew call you and tell you I was running your feral in the fights, and you came charging out here to stop me. So let's talk."

"Yeah, let's," Pablo said. "Somewhere a little more private."

"Fine by me." Julio nodded at one of his crew. "Take his gun."

The guy stepped forward. Pablo didn't move, but he didn't have to. His own men got in front of him, ready for a fire fight.

Julio didn't look as afraid as he should have. "If you come fight for me," he said to Pablo's men, "I'll let you work for me on the same terms as you did for Pablo. If not, I'll shoot you alongside him. You're outnumbered. You want to die tonight?"

Pablo knew full well that most of his crew worked for him for money. There was some friendship, sure; but in the long run, they worked for Pablo because he paid them well. What surprised him was not that two of the men immediately went over to join Julio and Zach, but that two of them stayed.

Julio finally drew his gun. "All right. Let's go under the trees."

"Wait." Pablo lifted his hands. "No, you two get out of here," he said to the men who'd remained with him. "There's no reason for you to die for me."

They hesitated, assessing the situation. "Go on," Pablo repeated.

The men in his crew were, in the end, practical. They gave Pablo apologetic nods and walked away toward the cars.

"I'll pick them up later," Julio said, motioning with the gun again. "I can't believe you're surrendering to me."

Pablo's brain spun with escape scenarios even as he let one of the men take his gun and started walking where Julio indicated. "You're my brother. I'm hoping I can talk some sense into you."

"Only if you can talk fast on your knees with my bullet in the back of your skull."

*Ay, Julio, I predict that you'll regret every one of those words.*

They stepped under the thick trees that grew so well in Texas hill country, the branches blotting out stars, moon, and lights around the big barn. Darkness made for terrific cover, and no one had been smart enough to bring a flashlight.

Pablo felt something brush past him, sensed a whuff of breath and the warmth of fur. The skin between his shoulder blades prickled again, every instinct telling him to drop and get out of the way.

He took a few more steps, threw himself flat on the ground, and rolled away through mud. He came to a stop on his back and saw something leap over him, wildcat limbs flowing through the darkness. The thug the wildcat landed on screamed, his weapon discharging, bullets flying. Someone grunted, hit.

Pablo heard Julio cursing, men shouting. More dark shapes solidified from the trees, sparks igniting in the darkness. Collars. Shifters.

The fight was swift and ugly. By the time Pablo scrambled to his feet, all of Julio's guys and Zach's were down, many of them unconscious. Julio was screaming, hanging from the arms of the tall Shifter with all the body art. Now that the guy was naked, Pablo saw that he was well and truly inked.

Julio tried to twist around and shoot Spike, but the Shifter called Dylan materialized from the shadows, took the gun out of Julio's grasp, and crushed it into scrap metal.

Pablo brushed off his clothes. His suit was thick with mud, and he'd have a bitch of a dry-cleaning bill. "What the hell?"

Spike's teeth flashed in the darkness. "Nate said you looked like you could use a hand," he said in perfect Spanish. "Or two, or ten."

"Thanks." Pablo said it briskly, because he knew that Shifter help wouldn't come cheap. He was a long way in their power now. They'd been right about this territory being theirs. Just because no humans realized it didn't make it not true.

"Did you stop the fight?" Pablo asked Dylan.

Spike answered, switching back to English. "Can't stop it. Rules."

"Don't be an idiot," Pablo said. "That feral's insane. He's never lost, and you'll have to pry him off the other Shifter's dead body. He has a strong instinct to kill."

Dylan dropped the pieces of Julio's gun onto the grass. "Sean's on it." He faded away so noiselessly that Pablo lost sight of him after the man had taken two steps.

"Pablo." Julio's bravado was gone, and now he sounded like he was crying. "Man, I'm sorry. I didn't know what I was doing—"

"Save it," Pablo said. "I felt sorry for you when Mamita died, but now I think I've spoiled you rotten. We got a lot to talk about." He was looking around as he spoke. "Where's Casey?"

Not there. Pablo accounted for the fallen, but Zach Casey wasn't with them. "He's gone after the woman," Pablo said in disgust. "Stupid waste of time."

"He wants to kill her," Julio said. "He told me he'd help me if I took him to the girl. He's going to do her and then kill her."

*Dios*, would this night ever end?

Spike at last set Julio on his feet. "Well, then," he said, another grin showing all his teeth, "we'd better get down there and stop him."

*** *** ***

The fight had grown bloody. Elizabeth watched, her throat tight with fear, as the wolf tore into Ronan, and Ronan tore into him in return. Blood coated the wolf's fur and lay black against Ronan's. Ronan's Collar sizzled and sparked, but he wouldn't stop fighting.

Eventually, though, the pain would overcome his adrenaline, and Ronan would collapse. When he did that, the wolf, unhampered by a Collar, would kill him.

Elizabeth had been aware of Spike, Dylan, and Sean retreating from the ring and disappearing into the crowd. But she couldn't worry about where they'd gone. She kept her gaze on Ronan and the fight that might take him away from her.

*No, no, no,* a voice inside her wailed. *Don't lose him. Don't. Lose. Him.*

She had to stop this fight. But how could she? The four big Shifters Julio had brought in as refs were surrounding the ring, and the fifth ref watched them warily. Elizabeth wasn't foolish enough to think she could jump in there between two raging Shifters trying to tear each other apart and hold up her hands for them to cease. Sure, they'd stop instantly.

The refs would grab her and throw her out before she could even reach them. The four Shifters weren't letting anyone or anything interfere with this bout.

Ronan had the wolf under him. He drew back his paw, ready to knock him out, but the wolf suddenly wasn't there. Ronan's swing kept going, and Ronan, tired, fell.

The wolf pounced on him, mouth open, claws ripping. Ronan rolled onto his back and grabbed the wolf in a deadly embrace, but the wolf was too strong, too fast. He ripped at Ronan's belly, Ronan bleeding from a dozen wounds at once.

Ronan roared his pain, his Collar white-hot. The wolf latched his jaw around Ronan's throat and bit down. Blood sprayed, and Elizabeth screamed.

She ran for the ring, damn the rules and damn the refs. At the same time, the one referee who hadn't come with Julio jumped in and tried to break up the fight. The other four grabbed him and nearly threw him out of the ring.

"What the hell are you doing?" the first ref yelled at them. "We have to stop it. The bear's done!"

"The bear goes down," one of the other refs growled. "It's done when he's dead."

"That's not what we . . ."

The four refs closed ranks and blocked the fifth from the ring. He swung around, boiling with fury, and took off into the crowd. Going for help, maybe, but would it come soon enough?

Elizabeth jumped up onto the circle of cinder blocks. The things had simply been laid on the ground, unattached, and they wobbled.

"Ronan!" she shouted, waving her arms to keep her balance. "Ronan, hang on!"

Ronan wasn't giving up. He was fighting on, but his struggles were weakening, while the wolf held on, jaw locked around Ronan's throat. If the wolf managed to tear Ronan's jugular, Ronan would die.

Because of her. If he hadn't been shopping in her store that night, Ronan wouldn't be here now, fighting to the death to keep Elizabeth alive.

She had to stop this.

"Ronan!" Elizabeth screamed. She cupped her hands around her mouth. "I accept the mate-claim!"

She wasn't sure what she expected—for him to suddenly burst upward, throw the wolf to the ground, shift, and sweep Elizabeth into his arms? She couldn't be certain he'd even heard her. In any event, Ronan was too busy fighting to respond.

But Elizabeth needed to tell him, in case. Ronan was one of the good ones.

"Ronan!" she shouted. *"I love you!"*

*Love you . . .*

Elizabeth put her hands on top of her head as she watched him, the man she realized she loved, die.

*** *** ***

Ronan felt the tingle of it through the agony of his Collar and the crazed biting of the wolf. He heard Elizabeth's voice, though he couldn't make out the words through the fog in his brain.

But he felt the magic. It wrapped around his heart and flowed through his limbs like heady wine.

*The mate bond.*

That sense of oneness with a true mate, which Ronan had never thought he'd feel—had started thinking himself fated never to feel it—threaded through his body and completed him. The click he'd felt when he'd first made the mate-claim now became music.

"Ronan!" he heard Elizabeth scream. *"I love you!"*

Like hell would he let himself die when the mate bond was filling him, while Elizabeth declared her love at the top of her voice in a barn full of Shifters.

She'd accepted the mate-claim in front of witnesses and given Ronan the greatest gift of his life. He had never heard the words, "I love you," from another being. Liking, respect, comradeship, even affection. But never love.

Elizabeth was the first. And he loved her back with intensity that shattered all pain.

*Fuck this.*

Ronan gathered the last of his strength, wrapped the mate bond around it, and roared with sudden power as he rose up to his full Kodiak bear height. He ripped the wolf from his bleeding throat, lifted the crazed beast in both paws, and threw him as hard as he could.

The Lupine flipped end over end, howling, to land in a crowd of frenzied Shifters. Ronan swung around, great paws moving, contacting with the Shifter refs who'd sprung into the ring to stop him. The crowd moved back, some cheering; others, who'd bet on the wolf, booing and shouting.

The fifth ref, backed by Dylan and Ellison, stepped up on the cinderblocks on the far side of the ring. "The fight belongs to the bear!" the ref shouted. "Ronan, of the Austin Shiftertown . . . *Winner!*"

Screams and cheers from the Austin Shifters. Elizabeth was doing a little victory dance on the cinderblocks, her feet nimble in her high heels.

Ronan shuddered as he landed on all fours, his Collar's sparks slowing but still hurting him. The mate bond, though—the mate bond was erasing the pain.

Before Ronan could reach Elizabeth, before he could shift and snatch her into his arms, a human male closed hands around Elizabeth's waist, lifted her from her feet, and started to drag her away.

# Chapter Sixteen

Ronan barreled out of the ring after them. Elizabeth kicked and flailed, the man holding her in a practiced lock. He had a gun obviously in his holster—he must have gotten past the weapons check at the door.

Where the hell was Sean? Nowhere, though Dylan and Ellison had started charging to Elizabeth's rescue. Too late. The man got her out of the barn, Elizabeth still fighting him.

Ronan passed the unconscious feral Lupine surrounded by a circle of Shifters, firelight from one of the barrels flickering eerily over the scene. There Sean was, kneeling beside the wolf, a shiny new Collar dangling from his hand.

Ronan burst out into the night. He hurt— Goddess, he hurt—but he was not letting that bastard take Elizabeth away.

He came upon them suddenly in the darkness, Elizabeth fighting her way out of the man's grasp.

"Zach," Ronan heard Elizabeth say, and then Zach's body was spinning, flying to the ground, as Ronan's paw smacked him.

"Ronan, don't kill him," Elizabeth said in alarm.

*Why the hell not?*

The human part of Ronan's brain, a voice far in the background, reminded him that Shifters were executed for harming humans. The Shifter that was Ronan only saw someone threatening his mate, and that meant no mercy.

Zach took the split second of Ronan's thought process to get to his feet, blood on his face. He reached for his gun, found his holster inexplicably empty, and ran. Ronan roared and ran after him.

He heard others coming behind, Elizabeth's voice holding fear, Spike and Ellison trying to get Ronan to stop. Ronan only smelled his prey, the man who'd dared put his hands on Elizabeth, the man who'd caused her to live for years in terror. This man would die tonight for touching Elizabeth—*my mate*—for daring to come anywhere near her.

Ronan caught up to Zach in a little clearing in the trees. Zach had no backup weapon, it seemed, because he'd grabbed a fallen branch and tried to use it as a club as Ronan came at him.

Ronan rose, rage and the mate bond giving him glorious strength. He roared his Kodiak bear fury, shifting as he came down to the terrified man.

Zach's face was pale in the moonlight as he faced a blood-streaked giant of a man with madness in his eyes. "Who the hell are you?" he croaked.

"Her bodyguard," Ronan said, and raised both fists to strike him down.

There was a *boom*, an acrid smell of gunfire, and the hot scent of blood. Zack looked down in surprise at his right side, which now blossomed a large red stain. Zach touched the wound, then his eyes rolled back. His body collapsed into the mud, and he lay still.

Ronan roared in fury, his Collar sparking, as he swung to face Pablo Marquez, standing calmly by, a black nine-millimeter in his left hand, right wrist in a bandage.

"That was my kill," Ronan snarled. "Mine as mate."

Pablo tucked his gun into the holster under his coat. "No, my friend. *I* am a cold-blooded killer. *You* are not."

Ronan's mate-frenzied bloodlust made him want to rip into Pablo for interfering with his vengeance, but pain from his Collar, the heady feeling of the mate bond, and Ronan's own common sense stopped him. Better still was Elizabeth running into him, throwing her arms around him, no matter how bloody he was, and pulling him close. Distractedly he saw Pablo relieve her of the big pistol she seemed to have acquired, but he decided to worry about that detail later.

His Collar stopped sparking and winked out.

"Ronan, you stupid, stupid . . ." Elizabeth's words gave out, and she simply hung onto him.

Ronan gathered her against him. He didn't care that he was naked, her enemy dead at her feet, with other Shifters and a human looking on. This was his moment with Elizabeth, when the mate bond in him connected to the mate of his heart.

"I love you, Ronan," she was sobbing.

Ronan kissed her hair, nuzzling the red streaks in it that he adored. "Love you, Lizzie-girl," he said. "My mate."

*** *** ***

Pablo also offered to dispose of the body. He gave Elizabeth an amused look as he checked over the Sig Elizabeth had lifted from Zach's holster in her struggle with him. "Remind me not to let you get close to me," he said as he unloaded the weapon and handed it to one of his seconds. "You have a gift. If you ever need a job . . ."

"No," Elizabeth said decidedly, and let Ronan lead her from the grisly scene. Julio Marquez was gone—who knew where, and Elizabeth didn't want to ask. She had no doubt that Pablo would gleefully claim that Zach Casey's territory was now his. He was not the kind of man who did favors without thought of personal gain.

By the time they reached the barn again, Ronan was staggering, and he collapsed at the same time Ellison broke out of the crowd with a Shifter medic behind him.

Ronan was in incredible pain, Elizabeth saw. He'd lost a lot of blood, his body torn where the wolf had clawed and bitten him, his neck bruised and blackened from the Collar's abuse. He needed a hospital, but the Shifters weren't about to take him there.

The medic cleaned the wounds and then ordered Ronan to change back into a bear, a form in which he'd have more strength for healing. Ronan groaned as he shifted, and three Shifters had to help him climb into the bed of Ellison's pickup. Ronan looked for Elizabeth, his gaze betraying so much pain that she climbed into the truck with him.

Ellison and Spike lifted a blue tarp over the pickup's bed and began to tie it down.

"Hey!" Elizabeth called. "Suffocate us, why don't you?"

Ellison pulled a rope tight. "All loads in Austin have to be tarped, and he qualifies as a load. Besides, I don't want cops wondering why I'm driving around with an injured Kodiak in the back of my truck."

Elizabeth understood his point. They positioned the tarp so that Elizabeth and Ronan had plenty of airflow, their skill telling her they'd done this before.

The tented truck bed was warm in the night, Elizabeth cuddling against her bear. Elizabeth held on to Ronan as the pickup bumped down the long dirt track, Ronan grunting in pain every time the truck hit a rut on the washboard road.

Elizabeth held Ronan close and buried her face in his fur. He smelled of blood but also of warmth and himself. She'd fallen hard in love with him, but that was not so surprising, she thought as she stroked him. Ronan had helped her at every turn and never asked anything of her. He never did, from anyone.

She was quietly crying by the time Ellison pulled up at Ronan's house and shut off the engine. Rebecca came running out as Ellison untied the tarp, Cherie, Mabel, and Olaf following. Mabel pulled Elizabeth into an embrace while Rebecca helped Spike and Ellison get Ronan out of the truck. Rebecca instructed them to put him in the Den—there was a big bed there, she said, and they wouldn't have to try to get him upstairs.

Ronan shifted back to human as he came to his feet. He tried to stagger inside on his own, but Ellison and Spike ended up half-dragging him between them.

Ronan groaned as he hit the bed. His face was wan from too much blood loss, the bite and claw marks again oozing blood. His breathing was shallow, his pulse too rapid.

Elizabeth and Rebecca covered him, and Rebecca brought out bandages and antiseptic. But who knew what was going on internally, or what damage the shocks from the Collar had done?

"He needs a hospital," Elizabeth said.

Rebecca shook her head. "The human medical world still hasn't figured out Shifters. They might kill him trying the wrong thing."

"We have to do *something* . . ."

Elizabeth broke off as the door darkened and Sean Morrissey strode in, the Sword of the Guardian on his back. Both Rebecca and Cherie jumped to their feet, eyeing Sean with similar looks of terror.

"No, Sean, not yet," Rebecca said, pleading. "We don't need the sword yet."

"I know that, lass," Sean said. "But you do need my mate."

Andrea stepped inside, her pregnancy evident behind her loose, light shirt. Without a word, Andrea came to Elizabeth, gave her a brief hug, and then sat on the bed next to Ronan. In silence, she peeled back the sheet, laid her hands on Ronan's bare chest, bowed her head, and closed her eyes.

She stayed in that position for a time, unmoving except for her brows drawing together in concentration. Cherie buried her face in Rebecca's shoulder. Mabel, next to Elizabeth, squeezed her hand. Olaf said, in his loud, child's voice, "Ronan will die?"

"No, lad," Sean said. "Not tonight."

The sword on Sean's back emitted a soft *ting*. Elizabeth's gaze went to it, but the others in the room didn't seem to notice. Maybe it was supposed to do that.

Andrea drew a long breath. Then, to Elizabeth's amazement, the big cuts on Ronan's throat started to close. As she watched, the wounds narrowed, dried, and fused, leaving long scabs in place of the chewed and serrated flesh.

The bruises and cuts on Ronan's face and around his Collar started to fade, and Ronan's breathing eased. After a long time, he let out a sigh and opened his eyes.

He looked around at the people who encircled his bed—his family, Elizabeth and Mabel, Sean and Andrea, Spike and Ellison—and he flinched. "Oh, this is embarrassing."

"Better embarrassed than dead," Andrea said, patting his arm. "Stop doing this, Ronan. I'm getting tired of patching you up." She started to rise, then winced and put her hand on her distended abdomen.

Sean was at her side. "All right, love?"

"Fine." Andrea rubbed her belly. "There's a lot of kicking going on down there. I think she wanted to help me and was mad that she couldn't."

"Oh, can I feel?" Mabel asked brightly. "I love babies."

Andrea let Mabel place her hands on her stomach, while Sean looked on, both fond and protective.

"Hey, what about me?" Ronan asked. "I'm the fallen hero, here."

"*You* are going to be fine," Andrea said. "You're good inside; the wounds are only surface ones, thanks to your thick bear fur. You'll have one hell of a hangover, but that's your own fault for agreeing to fight a feral."

"A fight I won, woman. You should have seen the other guy. What happened to him, by the way, Sean?"

"He's with Dad," Sean said. "For now. Dad will take him to Liam for debriefing in the morning."

"Poor bastard," Ronan said. "Better him than me."

Everyone started talking, weighing in with opinions about the fight or the feral, or asking for details about it. Elizabeth strode into the middle of the group.

"Out. Everybody, out. Ronan needs to rest."

Instead of arguing, they obeyed, to her surprise — instantly, quietly, and quickly. Mabel was the last to go. She paused to hug Elizabeth.

"Congratulations, you two. I knew you were up to nookie in here last night. I'll have a Shifter for a brother-in-law. That is so cool."

Another squeeze, a wave to Ronan, and Mabel banged out the door.

Elizabeth came to the bed. She started to sit at Ronan's side, then gave in to her emotions and lay down next to him, wanting his arms around her.

"News travels fast," she said. "Mabel wasn't at the fight — at least, she'd better not have been. How does she know what happened with the mate-claim?"

"All of Shiftertown knows, love." Ronan ran a bandaged hand through her hair. "Half of them heard you stand up and declare that you accepted me, and you'd better bet half of *them* got on their cell phones right away to spread the word. Matings are a big deal around here. Shifters love them, and they love to gossip. 'Course, now Liam knows everything too. He's not going to let me hear the end of it."

"Tell him to get in line." Elizabeth lost the rigidity that had been holding her up all night. "You almost died tonight. Damn you, Ronan. And don't tell me everything's all right, because you won. You almost *didn't* win."

Ronan kissed her hair. "I won because of you, Lizzie-girl. Because the mate bond wouldn't let me die."

"Mate bond . . ."

Ronan twined his fingers through hers and brought their joined hands to his heart. "I feel it right here. It means that you and I belong together, that we have a bond no one can break. I hope, in time, that you feel it too."

He sounded so quietly hopeful that tears stung Elizabeth's eyes. "I do feel it, Ronan. I love you. I've never felt like this about anyone before. You're funny and warmhearted and strong and brave and generous, and I love *you*. And wonder of wonders, you love me back."

"You bet I love you back." Ronan's eyes darkened. "You rescued me, Elizabeth."

"No, you did a lot of saving my butt. Andrea is the one who healed you . . . how did she do that?"

"Fae magic." Ronan said it offhand, as though Fae magic was a common thing to find lying around.

"Andrea's half Fae, and the magic manifested in her as a healing gift. Lucky for us. But that's not what I meant."

Elizabeth raised herself on one elbow. "You've done so much for me. All the Shifters have. I've done so little in return."

"No," Ronan said. "I've been alone a long time, Lizzie-girl. Even living here with Rebecca and taking in the cubs — I've still been alone." He released her hand and brushed the backs of his fingers over her cheek. "I'm not alone anymore."

Elizabeth pressed a feather-light kiss to his lips, her heart full. "Neither am I."

Ronan slid his hand to the back of her neck, rising into the kiss. They explored and touched for a little time, in the newfound wonder of feeling.

"You know," Ronan said, smoothing her hair. "I think I'm feeling a *lot* better."

His sudden, wicked smile made Elizabeth's blood heat. She ran her hand down the blankets until she found a very large bulge under them. "I can see that."

"Mmm, did you lock the door behind my nosy friends?"

"I did."

Ronan chuckled as he pushed back the covers and rolled his warm weight over her. "I knew I picked the right woman."

"You did." Elizabeth smiled into his kiss and wrapped her arms around his broad body. She was safe and warm beneath him, not ready to go anywhere for a long time. She licked his ear and then nibbled it.

"My bodyguard," she whispered. "My *mate*."

Want more Shifters?

Read on for a preview of

## *Wild Cat*
**Shifters Unbound**
**Book Three**


and


## *Pride Mates*
**Shifters Unbound**
**Book One**

# Wild Cat

**Shifters Unbound
Book Three
by Jennifer Ashley**

## Chapter One

*Heights. Damn it, why does it have to be heights?*

Diego Escobar scanned the steel beams of the unfinished skyscraper against a gray morning sky, and acid seared his stomach.

Heights had never bothered him until two years ago, when five meth-heads had hung him over the penthouse balcony of a thirty-story hotel and threatened to drop him. His partner, Jobe, a damn good cop, had put his weapon on the balcony floor and raised his hands to save Diego's life. The men had pulled Diego to safety and then casually shot them both. Diego had survived; Jobe hadn't.

Diego's rage and grief had manifested into an obsessive fear of heights. Now, going up even three floors in a glass elevator could give him cold sweats.

"Way the hell up there?" he asked Rogers, the uniform cop.

"Yes, sir."

*Shit.*

"Hooper's pretty sure it's not human," Rogers said. "He says it moves too fast, jumps too far. But he hasn't got a visual yet."

*Not human* meant Shifter. This was getting better and better. "Hooper's up there alone?"

"Jemez is with him. They think they have the Shifter cornered on the fifty-first level."

The *fifty-first* level? "Tell me you're fucking kidding me."

"No, sir. There's an elevator. We got the electric company to turn on the power."

Diego looked at the rusty doors Rogers indicated, then up, up, and up through the grid of beams into empty space. He could see nothing but the gray dawn sky between the crisscross of girders. His mouth went dry.

This cluster of buildings in the middle of nowhere—which was to have been an apartment complex, hotel, office tower, and shopping center—had been under construction for years. The project had started to great fanfare, designed to draw tourists and locals away from the heavily trafficked Strip. But construction slowed, and so many investors pulled out that building had ground to a halt. Now the unfinished skyscraper sat like a rusting blot on the empty desert.

Tracking Shifters wasn't Diego's department. Diego was a detective in vice. He'd responded to the call for help with a trespasser because he'd been heading to work and his route took him right by the construction site. Diego figured he'd help Rogers chase down the miscreant and drive on in.

Now Rogers wanted Diego to jaunt to the fifty-first level, where there weren't any floors, for crying out loud, and chase a suspect who might be a Shifter. Shifters were dangerous — people who could become animals. Or, maybe animals who became people. The jury was still out. In any case, they'd been classified as too dangerous to live with humans, rounded up into Shiftertowns, and made to wear Collars that regulated their violent tendencies.

Diego had heard that regular guns didn't always bring them down, Shifters having amazing metabolisms. Shifter Division used tranquilizers when they needed to shoot a Shifter, but Diego was fresh out of those. Rogers, rotund and near retirement, watched Diego with a bland expression, making it clear he had no intention of going up after the Shifter himself.

A high-pitched scream rang down from on high. It was a woman's scream — Maria Jemez — followed by a man's bellow of surprise and pain. Then, silence.

"Damn it." Diego ran for the elevator. "Stay down here, call Shifter Division, and get more backup. Tell them to bring tranqs." He got into the lift and shut the doors, blocking out Rogers' "Yes, sir."

The lift clanked its way up through the few completed finished floors, then onto floors that were nothing but beams and catwalks. The elevator was an open cage, so Diego got to watch the ground and Rogers recede, far too rapidly.

Fifty-first level. Damn.

Diego had been chasing criminals through towering hotels for years without thinking a thing about it. He and the sheriff's department even had followed one idiot high up onto a cable tower two hundred feet above Hoover Dam five years ago, and Diego hadn't flinched.

A bunch of cop-hating meth dealers hang him over a balcony, and he goes to pieces.

*It stops now. This is where I get my own back.*

Diego rolled back the gate on the fifty-first level. The sun was rising, the mountains west of town bathed in pink and orange splendor. The Las Vegas valley was a beautiful place, its stark white desert contrasting with the mountains that rose in a knifelike wall on the horizon. Visitors down in the city kept their eyes on the gaming tables and slot machines, uncaring of what went on outside the casinos, but the beauty of the valley always tugged at Diego.

Diego drew his Sig and stepped off the lift into eerie silence. Something flitted in his peripheral vision, something that moved too lightly to be Hooper, who was a big, muscular guy who liked big, muscular guns. Diego aimed, but the movement vanished.

He stepped softly across the board catwalk, moving into the deeper shadow of a beam. The catwalk groaned under his feet. There were no lights up here, just the faint flush of morning and the glow from the work lights down on the ground that the power company had turned on.

Diego saw the movement again to his left, and then, damned if he didn't see a similar flit to his right.

Son of a bitch — *two* of them?

A sound like the cross between a pop and a kiss came from down the catwalk the instant before something pinged above Diego's head. Diego hit the floor instinctively, trying not to panic as his feet slid over the catwalk's edge.

His heart pounded triple-time, his throat so dry it closed up tight.

What the hell was he doing? He should have confessed his secret fear of heights, gone to psychiatric evaluation, stayed behind a desk. But no, he'd been too determined to keep his job, too determined to beat it himself, too embarrassed to admit the weakness. Now he was endangering others because of his stupid fear.

*Shut up and think.*

Whatever had pinged hadn't been a bullet. Too soft. Diego got his feet back onto the catwalk and crawled to find what had fallen to the boards. A dart, he saw, the kind shot by a tranquilizer gun.

Uniforms didn't carry tranqs, and Shifter Division hadn't showed up yet. That meant that one of the Shifters he was chasing up here had a tranquilizer gun. Perfect. Put the nice cop to sleep, and then do anything you want with him, including pushing his body over the edge.

Diego moved in a crouch across the catwalk to the next set of shadows. The sun streaked across the valley to Mount Charleston in the west, light radiant on its snow-covered crown. More snow was predicted up there for the weekend. Diego had contemplated driving up on Saturday night to sip hot toddies in a snowbound cabin, maybe with something warm and female by his side.

On the other side of the next beam, Diego found Bud Hooper and Maria Jemez. Maria was fairly new, just out of the academy, too baby-faced to be up here chasing crazy Shifters. The two cops were slumped together in a heap, still warm, breathing slowly.

Diego heard footsteps, running fast—too fast to be human. He swung around as a shadow detached itself from the catwalk in front of him and rose in a graceful leap to the next level.

Diego stared, open-mouthed. The thing wasn't human—it had the long limbs of a cat, but its face was half human, like a cross between human and animal. Did Shifters look like that? He'd thought they were either animal or human, but as he watched, gun ready, he realized he was seeing one in midshift.

The Shifter landed on open beams on the next floor up, then its shape flowed, as it ran, into the lithe form of a big cat. Morning sunlight caught on white fur and the flash of green eyes. Snow leopard? It sprinted along the beam, never losing its balance, and vanished back into the shadows.

Diego heard a step behind him. He whipped around in time to see the flash of a rifle barrel in the sunlight, aiming directly at him. He heard the pop as his reflexes made him dive for the floor.

He came up on his elbows to return fire, but there was nothing to aim at. Whoever had the tranq rifle had vanished back into the shadows.

All was silence. Nothing but rising wind humming through the building.

Diego reassessed his situation. He had a Shifter running around up here, plus one asshole with a tranquilizer gun. Someone hunting a Shifter? Could be. The laws about humans hunting un-Collared Shifters—those Shifters who had refused to take the Collar and live in Shiftertowns—had loosened in the last couple years.

But this Shifter hunter had pegged Jemez and Hooper with tranqs, and was trying to shoot Diego too. Why, if the guy was hunting the Shifter legally?

Another pop had him rolling out of the way just before a dart struck the catwalk where Diego's head had been.

As he scrambled up again, the catwalk, loosened and dry-rotted from years under the desert sun, slid out from under his feet. Diego lunged at the nearest steel beam, the metal burning his skin as he tried and failed to grab it.

The catwalk's boards splintered and came away from the bolts. Diego's heart jammed in his throat as his body dropped. Splinters rained past him. At the last desperate moment, he got one arm hooked around a girder, and he hung there, stuck like a bug fifty-one stories up.

*Son of a fucking —*

He couldn't swing his feet around to get them back on the girder. His arm shook hard. He realized he still held his Sig in his other hand, but for some reason, he could not make himself open his fingers and let it go.

His arm was aching, and he was slipping. He was going to fall. Five hundred feet to the ground. Why the hell hadn't he asked to be put on desk duty?

Diego tried to swing his feet up again, but he missed the girder. The jolt of his feet swinging back down nearly jarred him loose. That's it, his hold was going. *Damn it, damn it, damn it . . .*

Two strong hands caught Diego under his shoulders; two very strong arms dragged him up and up, stomach grating on the beam, and onto the catwalk. Diego lay facedown on the relative solidity of a catwalk, drawing long, shuddering breaths.

When he could, he rolled onto his back, and found himself looking up into the white green eyes and ferocious face of the Shifter, again in its half-shifted state. A female Shifter, from the hint of breasts under the fur and from the sheer, strange beauty of her. She had a wildcat's face, and the morning light glinted on silver links of a chain around her neck.

Before Diego could find his voice, the Shifter spun away in another gravity-defying leap. She landed on all fours, flowing back into the shape of a snow leopard. Diego sat up and watched her, stunned by the beauty of the long, powerful animal running with inhuman grace fifty stories above the ground.

Another pop of the tranq gun had him on the floor on his stomach again, this catwalk staying in place. Diego raised his head, finger on his trigger. He heard a snarl, the leopard's angry growl, and then running feet, both human and animal.

Diego pointed the gun through the shadows, but he could see nothing. The rising sun showed that he was on this floor alone, though the footsteps continued above him. Lights approached on the road below, Shifter Division finally arriving, bringing a couple patrol cars and an SUV.

A blinding flash lit up the floor above him. Diego squinted through the spaces in the catwalks, aiming, but the light vanished as suddenly as it had appeared. The running ceased, and all was silent except for the patrol cars' sirens wailing below.

Diego lowered his Sig and was about to sit up when two feet landed on the catwalk in front of his face.

Two human feet, female feet, naked feet. Diego lifted his head to find two strong female legs, skin tanned from the desert sun, right in front of him. He looked up those legs to two strong thighs, with an enticing thatch of dark blond between them.

Diego forced his gaze to continue upward, over her flat stomach with a small gold stud in her navel to firm human breasts tipped with dusky nipples. He made his gaze move past *them* – though he knew he'd dream about them for a long time coming – to be rewarded by a breathtaking face.

The Shifter woman's face was strong but contained the softness of beauty. Her eyes were light green, a shimmer of jade in the darkness. Sleek, pale hair fell past her shoulders, and a chain with a Celtic cross fused to it glinted around her slender throat.

Damn. And *damn.*

She was definitely all woman, not in any in-between state now. Diego had never seen a female Shifter before. His cases had never taken him to Shiftertown, which lay north of North Las Vegas, and he'd only ever seen the male Shiftertown leader, Eric Warden. He'd had no idea that their females were this tall or this crazy gorgeous.

Her breasts rose with her even breath, and she expressed no embarrassment at her nakedness, didn't even seem to notice it. "He's gone," she said. "You all right?"

"Alive," Diego croaked. He dragged himself to his feet, trying not to look at her delectable body or to imagine what that smooth, tanned skin would feel like under his hands. "Where'd he go? The guy with the tranq gun?"

"I don't know." The answer seemed to trouble her. The man hadn't fallen, the lift wasn't moving, and no one below was chasing him.

"At least I've got one of you," Diego said.

"Wha—?" She stared at him, stunned, then her light-colored eyes flicked to the beams above, calculated the distance. Diego brought up his pistol.

"Don't try it, sweetheart. Get facedown on the floor, hands behind your back."

"Why? I just saved your ass."

"You're trespassing on private property, that's why, and I have two cops down. On the floor."

He gestured with the gun. The Shifter woman drew an enraged breath, eyes flashing almost pure white. For a moment, Diego thought she'd leap at him, maybe change into the wildcat or half Shifter and try to shred him. He'd have to plug her, and he really didn't want to. It would be a shame to kill something so beautiful.

The Shifter woman let out her breath, gave him an angry glare, and then carefully lowered herself facedown on the catwalk. Diego unclipped his handcuffs.

"What's your name?" Diego asked.

Her jaw tightened. "Cassidy."

"Nice to meet you, Cassidy," Diego said. "You have the right to remain silent." He droned on through Miranda as he closed the handcuffs on her perfect wrists. The Shifter woman lay still and radiated rage.

Diego's hands were shaking by the time he finished. But that had less to do with his fear of heights than with the tall, beautiful naked woman on the floor in front of him, hands locked together on her sweet, tight ass. The best ass he'd ever seen in his life. He wanted nothing more than to stay up here and lick that beautiful backside, and maybe apply his tongue to the rest of her body.

Diego broke into a sweat, despite the cool wind wafting from below, and made himself haul her to her feet. The Shifter woman's look was still defiant, but he couldn't help himself imagining crushing her against him to kiss that wide, enticing mouth.

Diego made himself steer her to the lift.

Not until they were rapidly descending did Diego realize that since Cassidy in her human form had come into his view, he'd not once thought about how far he might have fallen had she not caught him, and the spectacular splat he'd have made when he hit the ground.

# *Pride Mates*

**Shifters Unbound**
**Book One**
**by Jennifer Ashley**

## Chapter One

*A girl walks into a bar . . .*

*No. A human girl walks into a Shifter bar . . .*

The bar was empty, not yet open to customers. It looked normal—windowless walls painted black, rows of glass bottles, the smell of beer and stale air. But it wasn't normal, standing on the edge of Shiftertown like it did.

Kim told herself she had nothing to be afraid of. *They're tamed. Collared. They can't hurt you.*

"You the lawyer?" a man washing glasses asked her. He was human, not Shifter. No strange, slitted pupils, no Collar to control his aggression, no air of menace. When Kim nodded, he gestured with his cloth to a door at the end of the bar. "Knock him dead, sweetheart."

"I'll try to keep him alive." Kim pivoted and stalked away, feeling his gaze on her back.

She knocked on the door marked "Private," and a man on the other side growled, "Come."

*I just need to talk to him. Then I'm done, on my way home.* A trickle of moisture rolled between Kim's shoulder blades as she made herself open the door and walk inside.

A man leaned back in a chair behind a messy desk, a sheaf of papers in his hands. His booted feet were propped on the desk, his long legs a feast of blue jeans over muscle. He was a Shifter all right—thin black and silver Collar against his throat, hard, honed body, midnight-black hair, definite air of menace. When Kim entered, he stood, setting the papers aside.

*Damn.* He rose to a height of well over six feet and gazed at Kim with eyes blue like the morning sky. His body wasn't only honed, it was hot—big chest, wide shoulders, tight abs, firm biceps against a form-fitting black T-shirt.

"Kim Fraser?"

"That's me."

With old-fashioned courtesy, he placed a chair in front of the desk and motioned her to it. Kim felt the heat of his hand near the small of her back as she seated herself, smelled the scent of soap and male musk.

"You're Mr. Morrissey?"

The Shifter sat back down, returned his motorcycle boots to the top of the desk, and laced his hands behind his head. "Call me Liam."

The lilt in his voice was unmistakable. Kim put that with his black hair, impossibly blue eyes, and exotic name. "You're Irish."

He smiled a smile that could melt a woman at ten paces. "And who else would be running a pub?"

"But you don't own it."

Kim could have bitten out her tongue as soon as she said it. Of course he didn't own it. He was a Shifter.

His voice went frosty, the crinkles at the corners of his eyes smoothing out. "You're Brian Smith's lawyer, are you? I'm afraid I can't help you much. I don't know Brian well, and I don't know anything about what happened the night his girlfriend was murdered. It's a long time ago, now."

Disappointment bit her, but Kim had learned not to let discouragement stop her when she needed to get a job done. "Brian called you the 'go-to' guy. As in, when Shifters are in trouble, Liam Morrissey helps them out."

Liam shrugged, muscles moving the bar's logo on his T-shirt. "True. But Brian never came to me. He got into his troubles all by himself."

"I know that. I'm trying to get him *out* of trouble."

Liam's eyes narrowed, pupils flicking to slits as he retreated to the predator within him. Shifters liked to do that when assessing a situation, Brian had told her. Guess who was the prey?

Brian had done the predator-prey thing with Kim at first. He'd stopped when he began to trust her, but Kim didn't think she'd ever get used to it. Brian was her first Shifter client, the first Shifter, in fact, she'd ever seen outside a television news story. Twenty years Shifters had been acknowledged to exist, but Kim had never met one.

It was well known that they lived in their enclave on the east side of Austin, near the old airport, but she'd never come over to check them out. Some human women did, strolling the streets just outside Shiftertown, hoping for glimpses—and more—of the Shifter men who were reputed to be strong, gorgeous, and well endowed. Kim had once heard two women in a restaurant murmuring about their encounter with a Shifter male the night before. The phrase "Oh, my God," had been used repeatedly. Kim was as curious about them as anyone else, but she'd never summoned the courage to go near Shiftertown herself.

Then suddenly she was assigned the case of the Shifter accused of murdering his human girlfriend ten months ago. This was the first time in twenty years Shifters had caused trouble, the first time one had been put on trial. The public, outraged by the killing, wanted Shifters punished, pointed fingers at those who'd claimed the Shifters were tamed.

However, after Kim had met Brian, she'd determined that she wouldn't do a token defense. She believed his innocence, and she wanted to win. There wasn't much case law on Shifters because there'd never been any trials, at least none on record. This was to be a well-publicized trial, Kim's opportunity to make a mark, to set precedent.

Liam's eyes stayed on her, pupils still slitted. "You're a brave one, aren't you? To defend a Shifter?"

"Brave, that's me." Kim crossed her legs, pretending to relax. They picked up on your nervousness, people said. *They know when you're scared, and they use your fear.* "I don't mind telling you, this case had been a pain in the ass from the get-go."

"Humans think anything involving Shifters is a pain in the ass."

Kim shook her head. "I mean, it's been a pain in the ass because of the way it's been handled. The cops nearly had Brian signing a confession before I could get to the interrogation. At least I put a stop to that, but I couldn't get bail for him, I've been blocked by the prosecutors right and left every time I want review the evidence. Talking to you is a long shot, but I'm getting desperate. So if you don't want to see a Shifter go down for this crime, Mr. Morrissey, a little cooperation would be appreciated."

The way he pinned her with his eyes, never blinking, made her want to fold in on herself. Or run. That's what prey did—ran. And then predators chased them, cornered them.

What did this man do when he cornered his prey? He wore the Collar; he could do nothing. Right?

Kim imagined herself against a wall, his hands on either side of her, his hard body hemming her in . . . Heat curled down her spine.

Liam took his feet down and leaned forward, arms on the desk. "I haven't said I won't help you, lass." His gaze flicked to her blouse, whose buttons had slipped out of their top holes during her journey through Austin traffic and July heat. "Is Brian happy with you defending him? You like Shifters that much?"

Kim resisted reaching for the buttons. She could almost feel his fingers on them, undoing each one, and her heart beat faster.

"It's nothing to do with who I like. I was assigned to him, but I happen to think Brian's innocent. He shouldn't go down for something he didn't do." Kim liked her anger, because it covered up how edgy this man made her. "Besides, Brian's the only Shifter I've ever met, so I don't know whether I like them, do I?"

Liam smiled again. His eyes returned to normal, and now he looked like any other gorgeous, hard-bodied, blue-eyed Irishman. "You, love, are—"

"Feisty. Yeah, I've heard that one. Also spitfire, little go-getter, and a host of other condescending terms. But let me tell you, Mr. Morrissey, I'm a damn good lawyer. Brian's not guilty, and I'm going to save his ass."

"I was going to say *unusual*. For a human."

"Because I'm willing to believe he's innocent?"

"Because you came here, to the outskirts of Shiftertown, to see me. Alone."

The predator was back.

Why was it that when Brian looked at her like this, it didn't worry her? Brian was in jail, angry, accused of heinous crimes. A killer, according to the police. But Brian's stare didn't send shivers down her spine like Liam Morrissey's did.

"Any reason I shouldn't have come alone?" she asked, keeping her voice light. "I'm trying to prove that Shifters in general, and my client in particular, can't harm humans. I'd do a poor job of it if I was afraid to come and talk to his friends."

Liam wanted to laugh at the little—spitfire—but he kept his stare cool. She had no idea what she was walking into; Fergus, the clan leader, expected Liam to make sure it stayed that way.

Damn it all, Liam wasn't supposed to *like* her. He'd expected the usual human woman, sticks-up-their-asses, all of them, but there was something different about Kim Fraser. It wasn't just that she was small and compact, where Shifter women were tall and willowy. He liked how her dark blue eyes regarded him without fear, liked the riot of black of curls that beckoned his fingers. She'd had the sense to leave her hair alone, not force it into some unnatural shape.

On the other hand, she tried to hide her sweetly curvaceous body under a stiff gray business suit, although her body had other ideas. Her breasts wanted to burst out of the button-up blouse, and the stiletto heels only enhanced wickedly sexy legs.

No Shifter woman would dress like she did. Shifter women wore loose clothes they could quickly shed if they needed to change forms. Shorts and T-shirts were popular. So were gypsy skirts and sarongs in the summer.

Liam imagined this lady in a sarong. Her melon-firm breasts would fill out the top, and the skirt would bare her smooth thighs.

She'd be even prettier in a bikini, lolling around some rich man's pool, sipping a complicated drink. She was a lawyer—there was probably a boss in her firm who had already made her his. Or perhaps she was using said boss to climb the success ladder. Humans did that all the time.  Either the bastard would break her heart, or she'd walk away happy with what she'd got out of it.

*That's why we stay the hell away from humans.* Brian Smith had taken up with a human woman, and look where he was now.

So why did this female raise Liam's protective instincts? Why did she make him want to move closer, inside the radius of her body heat? She wouldn't like that; humans tried to stay a few feet apart from each other unless they couldn't help it. Even lovers might do nothing more than hold hands in public.

Liam had no business thinking about passion and this woman in the same heartbeat. Fergus's instructions had been to listen to Kim, sway her, then send her home. Not that Liam was in the habit of blindly obeying Fergus.

"So why do you want to help him, love?" he asked. "You're only defending him because you drew the short straw, am I right?"

"I'm the junior in the firm, so it was handed to me, yes. But the prosecutor's office and the police have done a shitty job with this case. Rights violations all over the place. But the courts won't dismiss it, no matter how much I argue. Everyone wants a Shifter to go down, innocent or guilty."

"And why do you believe Brian didn't do it?"

"Why do you think?" Kim tapped her throat. "Because of these."

Liam resisted touching the strand of black and silver metal fused to his own neck, a small Celtic knot at the base of his throat. The Collars contained a tiny programmed chip enhanced by powerful Fae magic to keep Shifters in check, though the humans didn't want to acknowledge the magic part. The Collar shot an electric charge into a Shifter when his violent tendencies rose to the surface. If the Shifter persisted, the next dose was one of debilitating pain. A Shifter couldn't attack anyone if he was rolling around on the ground, writhing in agony.

Liam wasn't sure entirely how the Collars worked; he only knew that each became bonded to its wearer's skin and adapted to their animal form when they shifted. All Shifters living in human communities were required to wear the Collar, which were unremovable once put on. Refusing the Collar meant execution. If the Shifter tried to escape, he or she was hunted down and killed.

"You know Brian couldn't have committed a violent crime," Kim was saying. "His Collar would have stopped him."

"Let me guess. Your police claim the Collar malfunctioned?"

"Yep. When I suggest having it tested, I'm greeted with all kinds of reasons it can't be. The Collar can't be removed, and anyway it would be too dangerous to have Brian Collarless if he could be. Also too dangerous to provoke him to violence and see if the Collar stops him. Brian's been calm since he was brought in. Like he's given up." She looked glum. "I hate to see someone give up like that."

"You like the underdog?"

She grinned at him with red lips. "You could say that, Mr. Morrissey. Me and the underdog go back a long way."

Liam liked her mouth. He liked imagining it on his body, on certain parts of his anatomy in particular. He had no business thinking that, but the thoughts triggered a physical reaction below the belt.

Weird. He'd never even considered having sex with a human before. He didn't find human women attractive; Liam preferred to be in his big cat form for sex. He found sex that way much more satisfying. With Kim, he'd have to remain human.

His gaze strayed to her unbuttoned collar. Of course, it might not be so bad to be human with her . . .

*What the hell am I thinking?* Liam's instructions had been clear, and Liam agreeing to them had been the only way Fergus had allowed Kim to come to Shiftertown at all. Fergus wasn't keen on a human woman having charge of Brian's case, not that they had any choice. Fergus had been pissed about Brian's arrest from the beginning and thought the Shifters should back off and stay out of it. Almost like he believed Brian was guilty.

But Fergus lived down on the other side of San Antonio, and what he didn't know wouldn't hurt him. Liam's father trusted Liam to handle this his own way, and Liam would.

"So what do you expect from me, love?" he asked Kim. "Want to test *my* Collar?"

"No, I want to know more about Brian, about Shifters and the Shifter community. Who Brian's people are, how he grew up, what it's like to live in a Shifter enclave." She smiled again. "Finding six independent witnesses who swear he was nowhere near the victim at the time in question wouldn't hurt either."

"Oh, is that all? Bloody miracles is what you want, darling."

She wrapped a dark curl around her finger. "Brian said that you're the Shifter people talk to most. Shifters and humans alike."

It was true that Shifters came to Liam with their troubles. His father, Dylan Morrissey, was master of this Shiftertown, second in power in the whole clan.

Humans knew little about the careful hierarchy of the Shifter clans and prides — packs for Lupines — and still less about how informally but efficiently everything got done. Dylan was the Morrissey pride leader and the leader of this Shiftertown, and Fergus was the clan leader for the Felines of South Texas, but Shifters with a problem sought out Liam or his brother Sean for a chat. They'd meet in the bar or at the coffee shop around the corner. *So, Liam, can you ask your father to look into it for me?*

No one would petition Dylan or Fergus directly. That wasn't done. But chatting about things to Liam over coffee, that was fine and didn't draw attention to the fact that the person in question had troubles.

Everyone would know anyway, of course. Life in a Shiftertown reminded Liam very much of life in the Irish village he'd lived near until they'd come to Texas twenty years ago. Everyone knew everything about everyone, and news traveled, lightning-swift, from one side of the village to the other.

"Brian never came to me," he said. "I never knew anything about this human girl until suddenly the police swoop in here and arrest him. His mother struggled out of bed to watch her son be dragged away. She didn't even know why for days."

Kim watched Liam's blue eyes harden. The Shifters were angry about Brian's arrest, that was certain. Citizens of Austin had tensely waited for the

Shifters to make trouble after the arrest, to break free and try to retaliate with violence, but Shiftertown remained quiet. Kim wondered why, but she wasn't about to ask right now and risk angering the one person who might help her.

"Exactly my point," she said. "This case has been handled badly from start to finish. If you help me, I can spring Brian and make a point at the same time. You don't mess with people's rights, not even Shifters'."

Liam's eyes grew harder, if that were possible. It was like looking at living sapphire. "I don't give a damn about making a point. I give a damn about Brian's family."

All right, so she'd miscalculated about what would motivate him. "In that case, Brian's family will be happier with him outside prison, not inside."

"He won't go to prison, love. He'll be executed, and you know it. No waiting twenty years on death row, either. They'll kill him, and they'll kill him fast."

That was true. The prosecutor, the county sheriff, the attorney general, and even the governor, wanted an example made of Brian. There hadn't been a Shifter attack in twenty years, and the Texas government wanted to assure the world that they weren't going to allow one now.

"So are you going to help me save him?" Kim asked. If he wanted to be direct and to the point, fine. So could she. "Or let him die?"

Anger flickered through Liam's eyes again, then sorrow and frustration. Shifters were emotional people from what she'd seen in Brian, not bothering to hide what they felt. Brian had lashed out at Kim many times before he'd grudgingly acknowledged that she was on his side.

If Liam decided to stonewall her, Brian had said, Kim had no hope of getting cooperation from the other Shifters. Even Brian's own mother would take her cue from Liam.

Liam had the look of a man who didn't take shit from anyone. A man used to giving the orders himself, but so far he hadn't seemed brutal. He could make his voice go soft and lilting, reassuring, friendly. He was a defender, she guessed. A protector of his people.

Was he deciding whether to protect Brian? Or whether to turn his back?

Liam's gaze flicked past her to the door, every line of his body coming alert. Kim's nerves made her jump. "What is it?"

Liam got out of his chair and started around the desk at the same time the door scraped open and another man—another Shifter—walked in.

Liam's expression changed. "Sean." He clasped the other Shifter's arms and pulled him into a hug.

More than a hug. Kim watched, open-mouthed, as Liam wrapped his arms around the other man, gathered him close, and nuzzled his cheek.

# About the Author

*New York Times* bestselling and award-winning author Jennifer Ashley has written more than 35 published novels and novellas in romance, urban fantasy, and mystery under the names Jennifer Ashley, Allyson James, and Ashley Gardner. Her books have been nominated for and won Romance Writers of America's RITA (given for the best romance novels and novellas of the year), several *RT BookReviews* Reviewers Choice awards (including Best Urban Fantasy, Best Historical Mystery, and Career Achievement in Historical Romance). Jennifer's books have been translated into a dozen different languages and have earned starred reviews in *Booklist*.

More about the Shifters Unbound series can be found at www.jennifersromances.com. Or email Jennifer at jenniferashley@cox.net

### Books in the Shifters Unbound series
*Pride Mates*
*Primal Bonds*
*Bodyguard*
*Wild Cat*
And more to come!

### Books in the Mackenzies series
*The Madness of Lord Ian Mackenzie*
*Lady Isabella's Scandalous Marriage*
*The Many Sins of Lord Cameron*
*The Duke's Perfect Wife*
And more to come!